A ROYAL PRINCESS

A Sweet Fantasy Romance

THE DANCING PRINCESSES
BOOK III

ALEA HENLE

CRABGRASS
PUBLISHING

ISBN: 978-1-952735-17-2 (e-book), 978-1-952735-18-9 (print)

Published by Crabgrass Publishing

Editing by Rare Bird Editing.

Cover design by Augusta Scarlett

❀ Created with Vellum

I

Nefeli longed to be anywhere but the heavy silence of the infirmary.

The surroundings offered the potential for serene rest and reflection. The room held a bed, small table for drinks and medicines, stool for guests, and a mosaic of fish decorating the whitewashed walls. Narrow windows in the walls and above the door allowed free circulation of cool evening air, whisking away all but hints of the medicinal tang inherent in the infirmary.

Breezes tugged at the hem of her soft yellow tunic and gold mantle, whisked along the sash that tamed the fabric at her waist, and ruffled through her close-trimmed black ringlets. She leaned against the cool stone wall and shifted her weight from one sandaled foot to the other, setting her bronze anklets chiming.

A lovely sound, because it was a sound. Likewise, she appreciated the trickle of water in the fountain in the plaza at the center of the infirmary, and the distant laughter and happy chatter from down the hall where a family gathered around a different patient.

Oh, to be among them or elsewhere in the palace.

Her brother, Todor, had asked a favor, which he rarely did. She granted it, and this was her reward: heavy, loathsome quiet.

A fitting punishment for not stopping to ponder why he wanted her with him while he visited his lover. He'd kept their budding estrangement too close a secret—Nefeli had caught no hint of it, oddly, or she'd have questioned his request.

Alas, she now kept company with two who studiously stared at their laps and said nothing. The three of them all as still and silent as blocks of wood—one of the land's magical Dancing Princesses, who guarded against natural and unnatural disasters, and two of the three royal-born compeers who partnered the princesses, and no one spoke a word!

Todor sat on a solid wooden stool. Informally clad in dark blue knee-length tunic and no mantle, or jewelry, he'd run his fingers through his black hair—a match for Nefeli's but without the curl—so many times that his hands bore half the pine-scented oil he used to keep it in place. His thin lips pressed tight together under a steep nose and thin black brows, his burnished skin warm.

He should have appeared strong and stalwart, a broader version of their mother, but the position diminished him. It reduced his height and breadth to the slumped posture that their tutors had tried to train out of him as a youngling. For his own good and protection, Nefeli had nagged him about it too. Their grandmother—their mother's mother —hated any such sign of weakness and slapped him whenever she caught him slouching.

Though grandmother never had much to do with him otherwise. Fortunate him.

Ylena, the princess Todor avoided looking at, sat straight upright despite an ample supply of grass-stuffed pillows to lean against. She'd pulled her blonde hair back into a loose braid, the ends trailed over her breasts beneath her simple green tunic. Brown eyes dominated a round face, glowing above a thin nose. Her hands clasped together, light beige fingers resting on her soft belly. A white sheet covered most of the bed, tented over the thick lengths of wood that held her broken leg straight.

A pair of crutches leaned against the corner near the hallway, oppo-site Nefeli and far enough away that Ylena couldn't reach them on her own.

A just reward, considering the other woman had walked across the palace a few weeks earlier, with her leg only partly-healed, and put her recovery back. Still, at least she was allowed to walk again even if only under strict supervision.

If Jola, Nefeli's lover, were in the same situation Nefeli would celebrate her returning health. Bring her favorite goodies, offer tales and reassurances. Cuddle with her on the bed.

Anything other than this heavy nothingness.

Todor's dark eyes flashed as he threw a pleading glance at Nefeli.

She'd seen that look before, though not for nearly a decade. Not since their grandmother's death from a strike of lightning . . . or a ball of fire fallen from the sky. No one was quite sure which except that her blackened body had been recovered and suitably buried if not exactly mourned.

So many years dead, yet the old woman's poison lived on. Even now, her summation of Todor rang in Nefeli's ears unbidden.

"Fodder for the troops. He'll never make an officer."

Harsh and extreme, but she'd got the core of Todor right. He showed no sign of leading.

Ylena on the other hand . . . She'd pursued, courted, and won him. Though, true, she'd done so with grace and honesty and given him time and space to choose. He could have declined, but Todor never had been good at saying no. Then again, he'd flourished as her partner. Her compeer in the dance, her lover off the dance floor.

Or so Nefeli had always assumed. Yet their postures suggested little of love, more of exhaustion.

Reason enough not to speak—but not for Nefeli to remain.

"Enough." She pushed away from the wall, dusting her hands. The clap of skin against skin broke the thick stillness. "If you're going to sit in silence, you don't need me watching you."

"No, don't go." The stool legs squeaked against the stone floor as Todor leapt to his feet.

"So you can speak." Ylena crossed her arms over her chest and clicked her tongue. "I was wondering if a fish had eaten your tongue."

"I greeted you when I arrived and you said nothing, so I thought you wanted quiet." Todor edged further away, blocking the door.

Nefeli leaned back in her former place and rubbed at a faint ache in her temples.

"'Well, I'm here,' you said." Ylena turned up her nose. "Some greeting."

"I promised to come, every day, and I've kept that." Todor said.

"Every day, yes. Later every day. At first you were here in the morning, now the evening. What next, you'll visit at night when I'm sleeping?"

"Why come when you're awake when you don't want to talk to me?" Todor stamped. Most people would see his foot hit the floor, guess at his sullen anger from the thud, perhaps even catch the vibrations in the air from the movement.

Those born to be compeers, such as Nefeli, got more. The press of his weight against the stones, and the earth below let her read his true feelings. Anger and resentment, yes, but mixed with fear and hurt.

Ylena's bed frame kept her from touching the floor. Nefeli received from her nothing but an awareness of her presence, her location. The imbalance led to nibbling pains on the side closer to her brother.

The princess lifted her chin, elbows tight against her sides. "I never said I didn't want you to visit."

"You didn't have to." Todor said.

"Pleasant as this all is, you hardly need me here for it." Nefeli left the wall again, but Todor shifted to block her. His anger subsided beneath a swell of fear and desperation.

His gaze never left Ylena. "If you don't want to talk to me, at least talk to Nefeli. To someone."

"I speak to everyone in turn." Ylena lifted a stoneware mug from the table next to the bed and drank deep. She coughed, or chuckled, as she cradled the mug against her chest. "I believe Jola wrote up a schedule to make sure that I'm never left alone for long. Two or three princesses or compeers visit every day."

"Do they bring you all the news?" Todor's shoulders slumped again, his body drawing in on itself. Although the movement opened room for Nefeli to slip by, she stopped at his side and rubbed his shoulder.

"They talk of little else. Who Danced with whom, who slipped, who messed up, who angered Amara and made her order everyone do a second practice." Ylena tossed back another swallow. "They tell me everything."

"So you don't need me for anything." Todor's shoulders rose and fell as he sighed. A ripple of hope surged within exhaustion where his feet rested on stone. "Not even word of the upcoming Erevestisi visit?"

"They especially talk about the possibility of a formal visit, since the Erevestisi haven't come this way in decades," Ylena said, eyes narrowing. "It's official?"

"Mother received the formal request from their Governing Council and has agreed to allow it."

"I hadn't heard she'd decided." Nefeli licked her lips to hide a smile at Todor's flicker of pride in having something truly new. "They won't get here until after the Court usually leaves for the fall progresses across the land."

"She's sending word tomorrow, once she decides how to host them, but it's certain." Todor stood taller.

"That's all well and good, but I asked you to find out one thing." Ylena stuck out her chin. "Do you have an answer?"

"Not the one you want." Todor's anxiety seeped into the stone and up Nefeli's legs. Bumps formed along her skin.

"Then what?" The other woman asked.

"A fault was found in the flooring, a plank with a slight depression."

"No." Ylena hissed, spine crackling as she straightened and glared at Todor. He stepped backward, filling the doorway. "No, someone tripped me."

His discomfort made Nefeli's bones ache. Her mouth was dry, and blood pounded at her temples.

She pushed the sensation away, focusing on the stiff length of Ylena's broken leg under the sheet.

"Mother ordered an investigation, you know that. But no one saw anything." He swayed, raising a breeze that whipped around Nefeli's feet. "The dance floor was crowded, and we were doing an elimination dance—the second in a row. Everyone was getting tired, and several people dropped out with aching ankles. It must've been the flooring."

"The flooring." Ylena thumped the mug down on the table and

glared over Nefeli's head at Todor, though her gaze seemed to pierce Nefeli as well. "Do you believe me?"

"Yes." He shifted his weight from one foot to another. The weakness in his voice matched the doubt emanating through his feet.

"Go away." Ylena said.

"What?" Todor asked.

"Leave." Ylena flapped her hand. "Go away. Anywhere I don't have to look at you if you aren't willing to believe me."

"But . . ."

"Go!"

Nefeli turned around. The evening sunlight had begun to turn orange with the sun's descent, and the shift made his skin a deeper bronze. Mixed emotions emanated from him in every way possible, so clear to Nefeli that Ylena had to be in little doubt either. "Todor, she asked you to leave."

"I don't want her to be alone." Guilt and relief warred on his face, and in his feet. He turned big, dark eyes on Nefeli.

She let herself read deeper than usual. Truth leaked into the stones, who shared it with Nefeli. This was why he'd wanted her company—not for him but for Ylena. He nearly floated above the floor except for a solid dose of awareness that Ylena might not mean it. No shame at all in having tricked Nefeli.

"I'll stay as long as she needs company." She clasped his shoulder, gripping tight. Some of his guilt over Ylena drained away, but he cast Nefeli a sideways glance and flinched.

"Such generosity." A sharp bark of a cough escaped Ylena. "I accept."

Todor's departure made the room bigger, emptier. Nefeli pushed the stool into a far corner but declined to sit. She stretched her legs and feet, then leaned back. The stones here were far warmer than the other wall, having soaked up afternoon sun, and felt good against the tight muscles of her back.

Ylena mirrored Nefeli's pose, except tilted back against the piled pillows. "What about you?"

"What about me?"

"Do you believe I was tripped?"

Despite the heat of the stones, a chill ran through Nefeli's veins. All the fuss, all the worry, and the official investigation—yet until this moment no one had asked her that question or even anything close. No doubt her mother's doing, as so often the case. Protecting Nefeli, perhaps, or from a fear of learning whatever Nefeli might know. "There was something strange in the air that night."

"Do tell." Ylena huffed. "There've been a lot of those this summer."

"True enough." There were three that Nefeli knew of: Ylena's injury, the lightning strike that had changed a famed outcropping of stone into unknown flowers, and the night that a fellow princess had healed her father through a Dance once thought myth rather than fact.

The latter two were magical—the first?

Swallowing hard, Nefeli met Ylena gaze for gaze. "You won't ever get the answer you want about your broken leg, not from Todor or any of us."

"Why not?"

"Because no one knows. Whatever happened, it was impossible." Or so Nefeli preferred to remind herself whenever she woke shivering and dripping with sweat from nightmares where she relived the dance —and dreamed she was the one to fall, or Jola, or both, breaking more than their legs.

"It wasn't impossible because it happened." Ylena said, waving a dismissive hand.

"Who would do it?"

"Who might actually trip me or who'd want me tripped, injured to the point I may never Dance again?" Ylena asked.

Nefeli shrugged.

"I can list dozens off the top, who'd see me brought down that they may rise. Any princess with ambitions to be Terparchon after your mother dies." Ylena held up one finger. "Or it could have been you or your sister, for you'll have to admit your mother would be a fool to choose Todor as heir if he is not wed to a princess capable of ruling." She raised two more.

"Or anyone who wants to see a princess other than you as my mother's heir, which widens the circle even farther." Nefeli set her hands on her hips. "It wasn't me."

A new silence fell on the room. The light shifted further, loosing orange and turning pink. Footsteps down the hall sent rills of happiness through the floor to Nefeli as the princess who'd healed her father left his side with other members of her family.

Nothing emanated from Ylena. Her lips pressed tight together, then she nodded.

Nefeli exhaled slowly, her own relief flooding through her.

"But you hardly welcomed me." The other woman sniffed.

"You're wrong about that. I admire your competence and determination. Always have." Nefeli inclined her head. "You're a great princess."

"You didn't like seeing me with Todor." Ylena inclined her head in the direction in which Todor had escaped.

With a hissing breath, Nefeli offered Ylena the greatest compliment she could: the truth. "It seemed to me you did all, or most, of the deciding. Todor went along. I hardly think that's a solid base for two who might lead the land."

Ylena opened her mouth, a gleam in her eyes, but Nefeli raised a hand and forestalled her.

"And do not say you resemble my parents. My father defers to my mother, yes, because the right to the throne comes through her—but he pulls his weight rather than let her bear the full weight of governing."

"I wasn't going to compare Todor and myself to your parents," Ylena said, head held high, "but to Jola and you."

"Jola is a princess, and the epitome of competence, but she is otherwise nothing like you." Nefeli straightened, fingers digging into her hips. Her teeth clenched and her temples burst back into full pain.

"You have it the wrong way around." Ylena wagged a finger at Nefeli. "You're like me. You go after what you want—and you wanted Jola. She goes along with you, just as Todor does with me, or did, but how much of the deciding does she do?"

"You know nothing of our relationship if you can say that." Inclining her torso slightly, Nefeli asked "do you need something for your pain? I would be happy to summon a healer."

"No need," Ylena lay back against the pillows, pulling her sheet up. "I thank you for your company, but I would prefer to rest."

"Of course."

Nefeli was half-way through the door when Ylena called after her in tentative tones. "I'm sorry."

One hand wrapped around the wooden frame, Nefeli glanced over her shoulder. The other woman seemed smaller in the early dusk. Tired, no doubt, and still in pain.

Though she hadn't said what she apologized for.

Nefeli didn't ask.

She swept out of the infirmary. Passed her guards in the hall, but they responded quickly and fell in a suitable distance behind her. Both had warded her long enough to leave her sufficient space.

Nefeli moved fast, impelled by desire to be away from Ylena and to not have to face anyone else until she recovered her equilibrium. She left behind Ylena's hard words about Nefeli and Jola, and pushed aside considering the implications of the hard silence between the princess and Todor.

Most of all, Nefeli sought a place to be alone, as alone as she might ever be. Space to move without the weight of other people's steps pressing against her.

Usually the summer palace offered her that much. A swathe of buildings spread in the form of the rising sun along the lake's edge, it was filled with quiet nooks, open plazas boasting greenery and water fountains, and the thick growth of gardens.

Her feet carried her across courtyards and through halls, a back way to the lake that she'd long ago memorized. No one stopped her, although more than one gesture—hands extended, smiles—dimly registered. Training allowed her to lock Ylena's words behind a calm facade.

Push them back. Set them aside for another day. Nefeli's relationship with Jola had nothing in common with Ylena and Todor other than that each involved a princess and their compeer.

Nothing.

A sudden gust of wind heavy with moisture whipped around Nefeli. She stopped and discovered her unthinking path had led her to an immense plaza overlooking the lake. The palace center stood behind her, the array of arches and windows separating the plaza from the great hall. Beneath her feet stretched an immense mosaic that covered most of the surface. Tiny squares and circles in jewel colors formed the image of the first Terparchon selecting her consort and naming him the Marchon to rule at her side.

Step by step, Nefeli passed over the oval frames around the central figures until she stood atop her ancestors with one foot on each.

The sun had set, but glorious pinks and purples arched across the sky and reflected off the waters. Light breezes danced about, bringing sweet scents from the myriad plants blooming on the terrace below the plaza.

So different from the night Ylena was injured.

The mosaic was open to the elements, rather than covered with a wooden floor for dancing as it had been that night. No musicians played nor did a crowd seethe around the edges, alive with chatter. The quiet let her appreciate the crash of waves against the beach below, and the call of birds overhead.

Flickering torches had lit the space, with little aid from a crescent moon. Nothing hung in the sky this night but the first of the stars, for the moon had yet to rise.

Nefeli didn't want to believe Ylena, not about her fall or her insinuations.

But that Ylena would break her leg in an elimination dance? Fall, yes, most people did but usually on their backsides or rolling and taking out a half-dozen others with them.

Accepting Ylena's surety of being tripped hardly required doing the same for her comparison with Nefeli. They were two separate accusations.

Nefeli couldn't say for certain where anyone had stood when Ylena was injured. So many had crowded the floor. Nefeli and Jola, Ylena with Todor, Nefeli's mother and sister with their chosen partners, and others beyond.

Rolling her shoulders, Nefeli stretched her arms and back. They'd done so many dances that night—court dances meant to show off clothes and jewelry and graceful movements. At the last they'd done the tachino, a fast elimination dance that mixed sections of intricate, exacting steps with spates of whirling, with an ever-increasing tempo.

Without any attempt at recreating the tempo, Nefeli repeated the steps. Memory recreated Jola's beloved form in thin air opposite her as she swayed and curved her arms in exacting steps where partners mirrored each other. Little chance there to lash out and trip someone, even if done at speed. This was all about demonstrating control and one's ability to keep time.

The whirling, on the other hand, required keeping balance and not getting so dizzy as to go astray. A foot could easily go astray, accidentally or on purpose, and knock another dancer off-pace.

A shiver racked Nefeli and she stopped atop the image of her ancestors.

It could have been a faulty plank with a dip. The tiles remained solid beneath her feet, but the wooden dance floor had occasionally creaked underfoot.

That was it. Ylena just didn't want to admit that for once she'd stepped wrong.

Except . . .

The slap of sandals against stone barely registered above the call of birds overhead—but Nefeli noted the approach. Only one person walked quite that way, or rather one body. More than one distinct individual shared the short, slight figure who rounded the corner and made straight for Nefeli.

Zora, Nefeli's youngest sibling, wore a blue mantle edged with thick gold-colored fringe over a cream-colored tunic, pulled in at her waist by belt of twined gold and copper links. A matching circlet topped dark brown hair pulled back in a braid. She rarely went anywhere without those signs of her rank, perhaps worried she'd be overlooked or dismissed as a child without them.

But anyone who considered her young and malleable failed to truly take in Zora's face. Dark brown eyes filled with intelligence shone to either side of a sharp nose and thin, mobile lips. Each person living inside her walked slightly differently and had overlapping ranges of expression, however the keen mind behind remained the same.

"Whatever are you doing out here alone? Shouldn't you at least have a guard?"

"I'm not safe here?" Nefeli waved a hand at the distant shadows of her guards over by the far wall. She had never been sure exactly how many siblings shared Zora's body—at least three or four, but their presences blurred together in a way that confused Nefeli's senses. This time, however, she didn't have to wonder who faced her, for that particular sister, the primary one, different from the others.

"You're one of the people who discovered that gardener who wanted to kill all born compeers." Zora waved a hand in the general direction of the main gardens. "No one's caught him yet, or if they have I haven't heard."

The reminder stung. Forget their limited success, no one had even considered that a fellow compeer was being poisoned for months. Worse, when the crime was suspected the poisoner had managed to escape beyond the senses of Nefeli and the other born compeers. She clenched her hands, a growl escaping. "He's run far enough, or is hiding in a thick enough crowd, I can't find his footfall and neither can the other born compeers."

"Then surely it's not wise to be so exposed." Zora twirled in a circle around Nefeli, footsteps light and graceful and completely lacking in magic.

"He can hardly poison me for standing here, and I will know when anyone approaches." Nefeli set her hands on her hips and tilted her head at her sister.

"Fair enough. What if he embroils others in his plans?"

"Again, I will know when they approach." Nefeli checked, just in case. No one, not even at the second or third floor windows with a view of the plaza.

"If they are strangers, yes, but he might suborn those you know."

"I am not without defenses." Nefeli said.

"Good. What about Jola?" Zora stopped whirling, back to the darkening sky and deep waters of the lake. The long fringe on her mantle swirled about her wrists and ankles.

"What of her?"

"I wonder at your allowing her to go into the city today."

"She's her own person and needs no permission." Nefeli pulled back. Her sister's wording stung, too close a reminder of the many times both had wondered at their brother's seeming to need Ylena's permission to do or even be. "It's born compeers who are his targets."

"You forget Natter worked here, in the palace. Grew his poisons in our gardens, where who knows what he saw or heard. Even those who rarely see you and Jola together know of your love." Zora grabbed Nefeli's hand. "If Jola were to be captured, endangered, what would you not risk to see her free?"

"She has guards when she goes out."

"Two, no less than any other princess—but no more either. Have a care for yourself and her. She looked quite distraught when she returned earlier."

"Distraught? How?" Nefeli stiffened.

"Oh, worn, tense, twitchy." Zora let go and shrugged. "You know how she is when she worries."

Nefeli did know, though she tended to consider Jola more as apt to startle than twitchy when ill-at-ease. Or worried. Jola had seemed so lately, though she'd settled in the last days. Extending senses wide, Nefeli searched for her lover. Many others occupied the palace buildings, not least her parents and other princesses and compeers, guards and servants, but even among the familiar crowds Jola's step was unmistakable.

No one lurked near her. She stood safe within their suite in the royal wing—but pacing back and forth. The weight of Jola's worry pressed against the floorboards heavily enough Nefeli couldn't miss it, although she tried to restrain reading Jola's steps to keep them on an even balance.

"I'll take your warning." Nefeli threw her sister a smile as she turned away.

"Have a care for both of yourselves." Zora said.

The younger woman stepped out of the way as Nefeli hurried off to see Jola face-to-face.

Jola later wondered if she'd somehow known when the winds of change shifted to blow her way. A harsh longing for home smacked her hard enough to dampen her eyes. But what home? She had so many—her family's home near the winter palace, her rooms in the winter and summer palaces, and the heart of her lover, however long that might last.

Wherever home lay, she was not there but rather out and about on business.

Dancers of all ages passed before her, none wearing more than a knee-length tunic bound at the waist with the tops hiked over one or both shoulders. A few let their tops fall, the younglings showing gangly, growing chests while the older boasted solider lines. Limbs twisted to the beat of drums and lyrical strains of flutes. Bare feet stomped against a stone floor worn smooth with the passage of centuries, skin in shades from deep, resonant browns to lighter beige and tinged with acrid sweat despite the cooling breeze of evening. Their hair, far fancier in many cases than their tunics, ranged from glorious falls of curls from high atop heads to tight-woven braids to short on the sides. One and all dancers gleamed as they shifted through patches of growing shadow in and out of the warm slanted light of a balmy evening.

The same light gilded Jola in her place of honor at the center of one of the stone benches edging the rectangular courtyard, turning her pale yellow tunic to a brighter shade except where it was covered by a lightweight mantle in a harsh green. The sandals were dyed yellow to match the tunic, including the straps wrapped around her ankles and calves nearly to her knees.

She sat with the section's elders at their insistence, as one of the storied Princesses whose Dances soothed storms, calmed fires, and encouraged crops to grow. Although she encouraged the elders to take as much space as they needed, no one crowded her. People rarely did, especially after glancing at the gold and silver cords bound around her waist and the matching strands circling her head, no doubt stark against her red hair and pale brown skin.

Which caught their attention more, the cords of her rank or her red hair?

Or perhaps the guards standing in the corners, their red livery bright enough against the gray stone walls that Jola couldn't miss them despite her trouble seeing at distances, and so very different from the tunics of the section's inhabitants, undyed or done in pale shades that were cheaper to buy and easier to wash than strong red.

All three—guards, red hair, and the twined gold and silver denoting princesses—were uncommon in the poorer sections of Yaras, the summer capital.

True, the stone walls of the buildings surrounding the courtyard were much patched where Jola had gotten close view, since she saw only blurs the farther away something was. Worse, the walls almost completely lacked the decorative tiled mosaics other sections of the city used to hide repairs. A few stretches of watery blue tiles marked one wall, suggesting it had once held a sizable panorama. Otherwise uneven stretches of light gray mortar or stones of shades other than the dominant ruddy gray told tales of damage and mending. Along the near wall, a series of dark lines indicated how high flood waters had risen in the wake of summer storms both recent and older.

At least the floor had mostly escaped damage. Some of the stones had settled lower than their neighbors, but none to the extent they posted a great hazard . . . as long as the dancers took proper care.

Still, the families and elders and section residents turned out in numbers. Those not dancing gathered in clusters around the edges as they tucked into the food laid atop trestle tables. The section residents themselves had brought platters of cold-roasted vegetables wrapped in thin coats of flour, bowls of pickled red and yellow peppers, and strips of dried jerky. These mixed with dishes of more expensive ingredients, including sliced starmeg with honey-drizzled yogurt, and heaps of redberries, contributed by Jola and her assistants.

Many of the residents brought threads and needles to work on mending, or knives and wood to whittle. The late summer evening hours were better for crafting, turning one's hand to some task, than hot midday—and many a parent could hardly spare the time to watch their children's pleasure unless they could also work.

During the occasional pauses in music, when drum and flute quieted, the clicks of needles and knives underscored the harsh breaths of the dancers.

Jola rubbed her fingers. They'd gone soft over the years. She no longer bore calluses on the tips from sewing or whittling though she could manage stitches or fine work. If needed, which it never was. The servants who tended her quarters allowed her the occasional project, but with side glances and shakes of their heads. *"You'd not catch me doing mending if I could Dance,"* more than one had let slip in her presence.

She'd rarely answered them, for it was too hard to explain what sewing meant to her. Nearly a decade with the court, ten years come winter, but she still remembered the days when if she didn't mend rips or tack up fraying hems she'd have nothing to wear. Nothing warm against the chill of winter, at least.

"Hah! Hah! Hah!"

The musicians stilled their instruments in their corner, as two dozen dancers clapped hands, arms high above their heads. They formed an almost-perfect circle. The littlest were a hair off, a step further in or out than the others.

So, too, Felix, one of Jola's two assistants, as they politely termed themselves when in fact they ran the dance exchange program in Yaras since Jola was present only during the summer. The tall, roundly-built man stuck half-in and half-out. The skirt of his light blue tunic fluttered just below his knees while the upper portion rose over his barrel belly to tie across one brown shoulder. Though he'd likely set his feet so on purpose. As a former compeer, who'd retired exhausted after several years of service partnering princesses, he had excellent balance, timing, and memory for dance steps.

Indeed, Felix's pose allowed him to meet Jola's gaze across the intervening distance. Most of the dancers were children, but a few parents and other older residents had joined them. No sooner had Felix caught Jola's attention than he inclined his head toward the eleee next to him. He'd introduced the dancers to her at the start, what was this one's name? Aksan.

Jola gave a slight nod. When Aksan danced, the air around them sometimes sparkled a little brighter. A minute breeze fluttered their short, straight black hair against a dewy light brown cheek, although the air was calm everywhere else.

Definite signs of potential magic. Here was one worth watching. This was why Jola had succeeded in obtaining royal funding for her assistants to rotate through different parts of the city, teaching those interested in learning court dances and learning the dances that the residents were willing to share with them in return. Others did the same in the other leading cities of Codaros, under Jola's leadership and coordination.

"We will identify dancers with the potential to become princesses, or compeers, so that they may be cultivated and expand our numbers and strength." That was the key argument—she'd seen the Terparchon and her advisers' eyes brighten at that. The court rarely had more than one or two princesses above and beyond the desired dozen with the Terparchon as the thirteenth. Too many princesses danced at most two handfuls of years before retiring from the strain.

The situation with respect to compeers was as bad or worse. Barely a handful were born gifted with magic that let them partner princesses and help channel the power flowing through the dance. Most were taught to mimic the born compeers; both burned out faster than princesses.

Jola had not admitted that part of her motivation was to find those who could become princesses or compeers and give them forewarning of what might lie ahead of them so that they could decide whether or not they wanted it.

The kind of choice she'd lacked, .

She trusted Felix to find a chance for a few words with the young eleee, and ensure they spoke with her as well.

But first, more dancing.

A slow measure that let the dancers—their numbers growing with the addition of more children—practice an intricate series of steps Felix demonstrated. A circle dance, made of twirls and bodies leaning this way and that. Lovely to watch, dizzying to do. A good third twirled all the way to the edge to drop and grab a drink or bite as they watched the dwindling numbers.

Then a second drummer joined the first as they set up a hard beat for a fast dance. Heads turned, arms flailed, and torsos arced until every inch of skin gleamed with sweat. The stones and earth beneath their feet carried vibrations, to the point the stone bench beneath Jola trembled.

She stood with the rest of the watchers, snapping their fingers in approval, when the dancers came to a halt. Aksan's chest heaved as much as any of the others. If they developed princess magic, they'd need to cultivate more stamina, but they smiled. Joy in dancing shone from bright brown eyes. Then they met Jola's gaze, and narrowed in speculation.

Small wonder that, when Felix offered them the chance to suggest the next dance, Aksan stepped forward.

"Show us how the princesses Dance down storms."

Indrawn breaths and gasps echoed around the courtyard. Aksan clapped their hands over their mouth and ducked their head.

Jola licked her lips, pressing them together to hide a smile. Felix and Jola's other local assistant, Dorcia, managed to look taken aback, although they too expected someone to ask sooner or later.

It was a rare occurrence when it *wasn't* asked. Indeed, someone had the last time Jola and her assistants held a dance in this section, a little over a year earlier. The audience likely included some who'd seen her dance before but people were curious, and understandably so.

Only princesses and compeers, current or former, watched princesses Dance magic in their underground chambers, where they eased the wrath of storms and guided distant fires to protect people. A pity, that only they stood witness to their workings—but a necessary precaution given the amount of power in a Dance, and the need to direct the power across distances.

Aksan tilted their head to the side, peeping up at Jola. She met their gaze and smiled. Perhaps they would someday join the princesses and find out more.

Until then, "I can only give you a hint of what we do. Show you how we Dance, although it will be lacking in power for there is no storm now to ease, or other disaster to avert."

Cloth dyed in bright greens and blues flashed to the side, by the entrance to the courtyard. Such colors betokened the arrival of other courtiers, people with the standing to buy and wear vivid shades. A familiar lanky form hovered in the shadows.

No one in court—or anywhere else Jola had seen—stood as tall and lean as Heron. It had to be the eleee, one of the six princesses who did not present as female.

Jola motioned them forward. The brown-haired, brown-skinned eleee princess wore bright green tunic and mantle. Another trailed in their wake, Princess Solon, who'd wrapped his shorter, rounder, and slightly older form in blues. His head gleamed pale yellow-brown in the light apart from a thin fringe of grizzled black hair. Neither wore a circlet, but each had cinched their waists with twined cords of gold and silver.

Three more guards in red tunics followed behind.

"Allow me to introduce princesses Heron and Solon." Jola strode into the center of the courtyard, turning around to glance at the whole of the assembly. "Together, the three of us will show you a little of how princesses Dance."

Whispers whirled around the edge of the yard as the other princesses joined Jola.

"You want us to Dance?" Solon asked.

Although he'd participated in other exhibitions, his face showed signs of confusion: wrinkled forehead, eyebrows drawn together. Had he not done this for long enough to forget? She drew up rotations for exhibitions and exchanges, but princesses and compeers swapped places around fast enough she couldn't keep up.

"Draw no power. Just move as though we were at practice." She tapped her lips with a finger, summoning memories of recent storms they'd Danced together, and the different roles each regularly took. "Pretend we're Dancing a storm. I'll be the flood waters."

"I prefer wind." Heron stretched their arms out. Their expression remained as inscrutable as ever. Although friendly and ready to accommodate most requests, they rarely relaxed around other princesses—Jola had never seen them at true ease.

"Very well, I'll be rain." Solon took a wide stance, eyes flickering as he glanced around. "What would you have done if we weren't here?"

"Vary between the roles." Jola tilted her head at her assistants. "Or asked Dorcia or Felix to join me."

"Ah. Dorcia I don't remember, but Felix and I Danced in ages past." Solon waved at the other man. "It was a sad day when he retired."

The earlier dancers scampered to the edges of the courtyard to rejoin their families. Many passed along the food-laden tables, indulging especially in the treats Felix and Dorcia had arranged.

The angles of sunlight sharpened, and the sky overhead turned orange-red. More of the courtyard lay in shade as Jola, Heron, and Solon formed a wide triangle in the center. They faced each other, backs to the crowd.

Felix took the drums, and gave three solid whacks.

Quiet fell.

Dorcia paced in a circle around Jola and her fellow princesses. Only the retired princess's demeanor marked her as different from the gathered citizens. Her plain, undyed tunic resembled theirs—though it also was exactly the kind of clothing princesses wore to Dance. The skirts swished around her calves as she walked, as did her long, gray-sprinkled black hair.

"What you are about to see is the kind of dance princesses do to protect our lands and peoples. Princesses take on roles appropriate to whatever they're Dancing." The other woman had a deep, resonant voice, well suited to public speaking.

Heron turned a circle, waving at the assembled masses.

"Others Dance rain."

Solon did the same.

"Or flood waters."

The growing shadows blurred the crowd, but Jola picked out Aksan and nodded at them.

"They Dance at the direction of the Terparchon. She cannot dispel storms or other dangers completely, no one can, but she can ease them. The princesses will show you the kinds of movements they do in Dances, but this is not a Dance. Remember that, and remember this."

It wasn't much of an explanation, more a taste. A tease—or a lure for those interested, those possibly developing powers, to seek out more information. Still, the speech and the sample dance offered the attendees far more knowledge about princesses than Jola had possessed when she was plucked to become one.

Dorcia's sandals slapped against the stones as she retreated to squat next to Felix. She took up a second drum and hit the rim with the heel of her hand. The sharp beat sent reverberations through the flagstones.

Jola settled into a low stance, half-kneeling. Arms crossed and head bowed, she snuck glances to either side. Blood pounded in her veins. Excitement tinged the air, giving it a fizziness she could practically taste.

Starting the beat, Felix laid down the steady base thrum of a threatening storm. Dorcia added less predictable, higher beats and riffs.

A sudden gust of wind whipped around the yard, eliciting gasps as Heron began to dance. Their feet traced a spiral path, racing high on his toes. Then they sank to full feet, and their whole body began to sway. The wind gust settled into a light breeze.

But Heron only played with the audience, hinting and teasing.

Solon followed suit as he joined with quick patter steps as he dashed here and there, allowing himself to be blown by the wind. A hint of moisture thickened the air.

Surely not power-driven, but merely the effect of the growing shadow and cool of night. Princesses rarely Danced in such small numbers. Jola had assumed they couldn't do magic alone, until recently when proven very much in the wrong.

She didn't want to draw power as she shifted into movement. Dropping to her knees, she undulated her torso as she crawled at an angle. Such would be her role if she were flood waters seeping, gathering, rising.

The floor in the underground chamber was much more forgiving, especially with magic at work. Her palms and knees started to hurt within moments. Rising to her feet, she kept her knees bent, maintaining balance with fingertips against stone, body crouched low. Head bowed, too, which made it harder to track Heron and Solon, even from the corners of her eyes.

Usually her regular partner, her compeer, her beloved Nefeli, would be at her side ensuring she didn't get so caught up in the Dance--or, worse, make a sudden movement that blurred her eyesight—so that she bumped into someone else and worked unintended havoc.

Jola always missed Nefeli when attending a dance exchange. They'd tried having her accompany Jola at the start, but it never worked out. Being of royal blood, Nefeli required twice as many guards in attendance resulting in too much silence and awe, or resentment.

Even without Nefeli's care, Jola tracked her fellow dancers' steps enough to avoid them.

But she couldn't miss the soft mist forming in the air. A few drops of water splattered against the stones waking remembrance of past storms. A hint of power trickled up through her sandals and fingers.

A sour taste filled her mouth, a hint of blocked sewers spilling into streets and tainting the the rush of flood waters. She couldn't spit in the middle of a dance, nor could she bear to swallow. Instead, she bent her head and hid her face in the crook of her shoulder. Wiped her lips and tongue against her mantle.

A happy crumb left from an early pastry, stuck to her mantle with a whole drop of honey, broke the sour—and woke her to realization of what was happening.

One more wrong step, and they'd Dance a storm into being, or a flood.

Not acceptable. Gritting her teeth, she refused to allow power to recreate any past disaster. She drew in a deep breath. Rolled herself up to her full height and held her chin high.

Magic overlaid the physical world. Every movement of the dance—hers, Heron's, and Solon's—reminded the courtyard of what had been and might someday be again. Power flowed from their bodies. She leapt and twirled in a circle around the other princesses. She waved and bent and gathered the magic until, arms crossed over her chest and hands curved upward, she held a bouquet of power.

Only to freeze. What could she do with it? In Dances she never had to worry. Nefeli inevitably partnered her and soothed away any excess. Returned it to the earth.

Jola had not Nefeli's gift. Still, she bent and laid the burden on the stones. There it sat for a long moment before they accepted it.

Energy flowed through her blood and lingered in her bones, but the magic was dispelled. It all happened so fast she barely took it in, then pushed the memories away for consideration later.

A dull pain pulsed at her temples and she swayed.

The snapping applause worsened the throbbing. She must have paled or otherwise shown signs of power-fatigue. Felix rushed to her side, sweeping her away to a far corner. Comforting walls rose high on two sides, dark gray stones missing mortar here and there. The high water marks of previous floods shone faintly. Jola turned away, head down, and stared at the leather sandals wrapping Felix's hairy feet.

Dorcia's carrying tones echoed in Jola's skull as the former princess took her place answering questions.

Jola shivered as Felix handed her a cloth dripping with cool water. She pressed it against her forehead, waving off the former compeer's offer of a drink. Sweat poured down her, making her tunic stick to her sides. The cool did, at least, ease the ache in her head, as did the absence of the drums.

"What was that?" Heron tended a pale, shaky Solon, giving him a similar cloth. The taller princess's form helped block the audience's view of Jola and Solon.

"I've never seen more than a hair of magic at these, or we'd not hint at Dancing." Felix proffered a second cool, sopped cloth in place of the first. "This is a first."

"The stones remember." Jola accepted the new, cooler fabric and rubbed down her face and neck. The pain receded, although an ache lingered along her neck. She caught Solon's gaze. He reddened and turned his head downward.

"Hmm. Wonder if this is some kind of anniversary." Felix touched one of the fading marks.

"Perhaps our being here is encouraging the stones to remember." Heron did likewise. Although Felix's hand remained unstained after touching the wall, Heron's fingers glowed.

"Might be." Felix said.

"My fault." As Solon shivered, a few more raindrops coalesced and pattered against the stones. "I remembered. Woke the stones."

Jola froze, as did the others. He'd slipped into Dancing and tugged the others as well.

Solon's head hung low and shoulder slumped.

Although she'd earthed the power, a few sparkles lurked in the walls around them.

"We'd best go, all of us." She waited for Heron and Solon's nods, then turned to Felix. "Make our apologies, please? And don't stay, or keep anyone here, if the light and power doesn't fade with our going."

"I'll swab the place down if necessary." Felix clasped her hands, pulling her to her feet. "I remember enough cleansing steps for that."

The magic mostly subsided as they left, the air returning to cool with a hint of moisture. Occasional sparks flared around Solon, turning to drops of water that his tunic soaked up.

No stranger got near enough to notice, thanks to the guards falling in around them. Their stalwart bodies and stern expressions kept the crowds filling the street at a distance and ensured a path cleared. Though the nearest guards glanced at Solon several times, and exchanged pointed looks that presumably passed to those farther ahead and behind.

Shopkeepers opened their shutters for brisk evening business, calling to passers-by to come buy food, clothing, and the best of this or that. Wandering vendors likewise hawked their wares. Those who lived or worked in the upper floors ventured onto the balconies to eat, drink, and socialize. Sweet and savory scents mingled—turning Jola's stomach.

Her sandals slapped against the uneven cobblestones, keeping a steady pace. Usually she'd walk in the center. This time, Heron matched her stride on Solon's far side.

Solon had created raindrops and nearly called a flood from the stones—without intention. No need to ask what that meant: he verged on burnout.

He had to have recognized the danger signs even if no one else had noticed, for it to get this bad. Perhaps he had pushed them aside or even forgotten? Memory loss was usually one of the first symptoms of burnout and he'd seemed to have forgotten participating in other exhibitions. Trouble controlling power came later, or not.

"How long have you known?" She kept her voice low and words open to interpretation by any who wasn't familiar with princess magic.

"I wanted one last year, one last cycle to travel and see all of Codaros again before I retire." Solon brushed at a few last drops falling on his tunic, but the damp fabric soaked them up.

"You can travel after." So he'd seen warning signs a season or two earlier, for he, like Jola, was born and raised in Tharos, near the winter palace.

"It won't be the same." Solon's sandaled feet thudded hard against the stones. "My family are traders. I know."

A cough escaped Heron, who nodded agreement. They'd served a foreign government as a messenger before the Terparchon offered them a place among the princesses.

Jola had to take their word for it. She'd only ever traveled with the court as it meandered from city to city while moving from the winter palace to the summer and back again.

"I've been a princess near nineteen years, before all of you except the Terparchon and Amara. Longer than most. Didn't think the stones would remember. Wanted to go out on my own terms."

Jola could respect that, but only so long as he didn't endanger the rest in the process. The tall gray gates of the summer palace, flecked with metals that gleamed in the setting sun, loomed as they drew closer. Although not home, they offered shelter and comfort. "How close are you?"

"I'm good for what's left of the summer, since there's not likely to be any more storms here. I can handle fall, too. We don't Dance much on progress anyhow. But winter . . . the Terparchon will need to replace me then."

"You sure you can make it?" Heron asked, beating Jola by a moment.

"Yes, but . . . No more exhibitions." Solon waved a hand at Jola. "Sorry."

"I'll keep that in mind." She'd no mind to risk a repeat of the near-disaster, though there weren't any more exhibitions scheduled before the court left. "You've told the Terparchon?"

"Amara knows." Solon's voice broke on the admission.

And what the Terparchon's aide, a former princess in her own right, knew she shared with the Terparchon. No one told Amara anything unless they were prepared for that.

Heron laid an arm across Solon's shoulder, letting the man lean against them as they approached the gates.

Jola's steps slowed. She slipped behind them, the better to keep her expressions and thoughts to herself.

Nineteen years Solon had Danced, one of the longest terms. Jola only boasted half as long. Too many started and stopped in that shorter time frame.

Burned out.

Such wrongness, that they flamed and crumbled to embers so fast with few exceptions.

How much longer did she have? She'd had no memory issues that she knew, but her strange vision and earthing might count as trouble controlling magic. In which case she, too, was at risk. The muscles in her arms quivered and bumps rose along her skin at fears over what might happen when she no longer ranked as a princess.

A fierce longing for home swelled within her—but this time she had no doubts as to which home she wanted: the arms of her lover.

Jola's place as a princess might be part of her attraction for Nefeli. Losing the one could well mean loss of the other. Still, she would enjoy their closeness as long as it lasted.

$$\maltese \quad 3 \quad \maltese$$

The distant patter of Jola's pacing echoed along Nefeli's arms and legs. Much as she wished to match it, she maintained a slower pace.

A walk, not a run.

Moving fast risked rousing unease. Many of the court remembered the summer of the coup. The sight of someone running always attracted attention, particularly if it was one of the royal family.

Thankfully, the fall of twilight and cool air had lured most of the palace denizens out into the courtyards and plazas. Even many of the lurkers and pouncers had gone out, leaving the halls free of those members of court prone to snatching any chance closer acquaintance.

Nefeli nodded and smiled as she whisked her way to a narrow back stairway. Set into the exterior wall of the palace, the stones retained the heat of the day. The air remained close, hot and humid and harder to breathe than outside. Sweat beaded her forehead and lined her limbs, so she slowed her progress.

Thuds against her skin warned her before the sounds reached her ears of someone barreling downward. A youngling stopped on the landing, swaying with the suddenness. A page, light of skin and with short brown curls, they wore a simple knee-length tunic fastened over one shoulder. The particular twist of red ribbons looped at the shoulder indicated they served her father.

They shifted to the side, leaving space for her to pass—but fanned their fingers showing a piece of paper within.

She accepted it with a nod. Her father's handwriting was unmistakeable, all slants and heavy angles. She tucked it under the sash at her waist rather than slow to read it.

All the while, she tracked Jola pacing. So tempting to read deeper, to take in some of the feelings as the other woman's feet came in contact with the floor. Just a little, only enough for advance warning as to what troubled her lover.

Giving Nefeli an unfair advantage. Tough to resist, but she managed. She'd promised Jola when they first laid together, bodies entwined, that she wouldn't abuse her ability to know more about Jola than the princess could learn about her. Jola hadn't asked, but Nefeli hadn't missed the relief in her eyes.

Or what she thought was relief, since she'd started keeping her promise immediately.

If Nefeli hadn't offered, would Jola have asked? The princess had impressed Nefeli from the first with her determination to do well at whatever task lay before her. Yet despite years of demonstrating quiet competence that earned respect from all who knew her, Jola rarely asked for anything from Nefeli save due time and attention.

It was Nefeli who had made the first moves.

She darted through the door, letting it slam behind her. The wall baskets with luminescent stones filled the room with bright light and sharp shadows. No signs of anything amiss—blue lounging couches in their usual place near the window, shutters thrown open to let in the cool breeze, a tray of water and light sweets on the table between the cloth-over-straw-and-wood-frame couches—then Jola turned to face her and the room became a blur. Only Jola mattered.

The princess's composure struck Nefeli as always. Tall and slender, Jola shifted easily between stillness and sudden movement. Her arms pressed tight against her side, wrinkling the yellow and green of her tunic and mantle. Many of the court chuckled over her choice of clothes and colors behind her back and before her face, but she only smiled and did as she pleased. She chose colors because she liked them, not to make a pretty picture for others.

Sometimes Jola struck Nefeli as a glorious bird proud of its plumage and uncaring of criticism, albeit a bird without much of a beak. Jola's face was round and decidedly moon-like, with lines at her eyes from squinting to see at distances. This, combined with her clothes, contributed to people underestimating her. Yet get close, and the keen intelligence within shone through.

A faint musty smell hung about her as though she'd been in murky waters. The hem of her mantle showed signs of water stains.

Still, a glad smile stretched Jola's thin lips at the sight of Nefeli. Shifting from stillness, she rushed over pausing only long enough to Nefeli to nod before clutching her close.

Jola's hands pressed against Nefeli's back as she bent and tucked her head against Nefeli's neck. Nefeli slipped her arms around Jola's waist, easy given their relative heights.

No matter how Nefeli tried, she couldn't completely shut down awareness of much of Jola's tension slipping away. Her lover's stance shifted, weighing lighter against the floor. Likewise, the muscles of her back eased under Nefeli's fingers.

"Are you all right?" Nefeli asked.

"How did you know I needed you?" Jola's lips moved against Nefeli's shoulder, words muffled but audible.

"Zora brought word."

"Zora! I didn't see her at all." Jola pulled back to the edge of Nefeli's embrace, blinking and shaking her head. "She saw me?"

"Said you looked troubled." Nefeli bent and ran a hand along the hem of Jola's mantle. The once-soft fabric was dry but stiff. Here and there clods of dirt or other matter clung to the loose woven threads.

"I'm unharmed." Jola twitched her mantle from Nefeli's grasp.

"But not untouched."

"We nearly caused a flood at the dance exhibition earlier. Solon lost control." Jola sank onto a sofa, lifting her mantle and studying the hem with her head tilted to the side. "I felt the ghost rain he brought, but missed that. I'd best put it to soak."

Smiling at Nefeli, Jola leapt back to her feet and scooted over into bedroom. Her footsteps echoed in Nefeli's ears and along her skin as her lover continued across the room. Water trickled as Jola no doubt filled the bowl from the pitcher, and then the soft whoosh of Jola immersing the fabric.

Nefeli would have dropped the mantle in the laundry pile for someone else to worry over, but Jola always did more than needed. Tidied the room, dusted, even fetched water on occasion.

Sticky and still damp with sweat, Nefeli doffed her mantle. The breeze tugged at her tunic and cooled her. She hung the lightweight swathe of fabric on a peg near the bedroom door, next to the laundry basket though it likely wouldn't need much more than a good brushing. Jola's trim form was visible beneath her thin tunic as she worked over the mantle.

Returning to the outer room, Nefeli noted a tray on the low table between couches. Condensation dripped down the sides of the red clay jug, containing cider by the sharp, clean aroma. Two mugs rested nearby. A light cloth with red stones sewn into the corners to keep it from being blown away covered a plate. She lifted a corner, and slipped out a slice of melon to snack on.

Something crackled as she settled onto a couch. The paper passed to her earlier had new folds when she fished it out, but remained legible.

Her father wanted her to meet him early the next morning, naming a room she didn't remember at first sight or second thought. No word of what or why. Even with her grandmother dead a decade, he remained chary about trusting anything to paper that might come back to bite him.

At least he didn't want to meet until morning. She could relax with Jola first. Rising from the couch, she made a circle around the room closing half of the hanging baskets with luminescent stones for a softer glow.

Only to stop and stare at the last, hands still resting on the wicker top.

The mere fact Jola had opened all of them said something about her earlier troubles, the exact nature of which Nefeli's lover had yet to truly share. But Nefeli couldn't push, that would make her more like Ylena with Todor.

Damn Ylena for raising the possibility in the first place.

J ola paused in the doorway, hands still damp. Her tunic flowed
loose around her, for she'd removed sash and jewelry as well as
mantle. She moved in silence, unlike Nefeli who'd taken off only
her mantle. Bracelets and anklets jingled as Jola's lover proceeded
from one light basket to another.

Fitting that a woman whom no one could sneak up on chose to
make sounds whenever she moved. Though Nefeli was hard to ignore
under any circumstance. Jola'd heard people describe her lover as solid,
formidable. A statue or a stone wall. But they reacted not so much to
her body as to the way she melded with whatever surface she stood or
sat upon. Nefeli could not be moved unless she wished to be. When
she did wish, her dark eyes flashed, mobile mouth straightened, and
she might force through a stone wall.

On closer look, for those who cared and those for whom she cared,
she was a hillside in full spring bloom, a sight Jola never tired of. Nefeli's high, curved cheeks flushed hot and pink-tinged when happy. Her
steep nose whose tip twitched when she made a joke, above broad lips
made for smiling. Her feet were capable of tracing intricate dance
steps all night.

Too few people went beyond Nefeli's solidity to consider how easily she might be hurt.

Then again, Nefeli contributed to that. She rarely stood in full sunlight. Given a choice, she'd have at most half the light baskets open in any given room. Even at brightly lit court affairs, she managed to find points of shadow most particularly in her mother's wake.

Jola regularly opened all the light baskets in the room to give Nefeli something to do.

With half the baskets open, the light had a muted quality. Overlapping shadows filled the corners. The soft calls of night birds soaring over the lake or gardens echoed in the distance. Nefeli's rooms overlooked the children's palace, the small palace-within-the-palace where the children of courtiers and servants played and studied. By day, it was noisy, but at night when most children had gone to spend time with their parents, quiet and lovely.

A true retreat from the cares of the world, except when they followed one home.

Jola sighed and crossed the floor to the couches. A floor board creaked despite the soft covering rug, but no matter. Nefeli knew where Jola was anyway.

"Cider?" Jola filled a mug half-way for herself and held the jug over the second.

"Yes." Nefeli reclined on the other couch and took a deep draft.

Settling opposite, Jola did the same. The sweet, sharp drink still held a soothing hint of chill.

The couches sat at angles, positioned close enough that, even with the table in the corner, they could easily lean in and kiss.

Before thought turned to action, a breeze gusted in through the bedroom and brought a hint of murky flood waters with it. Wiping with a damp cloth was not enough. Jola's mantle would need full laundering to be truly clean.

That, at least, was easier than what Solon faced.

And, perhaps, Jola as well. Her head hung low, chin against her chest.

"What went wrong?" Nefeli leaned over and squeezed Jola's hand, bracelets brushing her arm. Then she pulled back, an odd expression flickering across her face. "Tell me all you will."

Tell all, tell some . . . Jola slid down the couch so she lay flat except for her calves and feet which dangled off the end. Her hands slid off to hang as well. "Solon's burning out."

"Another." Nefeli reached across and tangled her fingers with Jola's. "He's lasted longer than most."

"Twenty years." Jola grabbed tight when Nefeli seemed to pull away. "Most of us don't make ten. Amara, Dacia, Yanna . . . Near all those who started Dancing before me have retired or flamed out. Only Melite remains, and she has only a few months on me. All the other princesses have less than eight years." She rose to a seated position and swung her legs around, still holding Nefeli's hand. "Doesn't that strike you as strange, that so many Dance so few years?"

"It's a hard life. It takes a toll, and not everyone can manage it. Compeers burn out as fast or faster." Nefeli snarled, teeth flashing, then she turned to match Jola's pose and grabbed her other hand. "Are you . . ."

Nefeli didn't shape the words, but she didn't have to.

"I don't know." Jola pulled one hand free and grabbed her mug, downing the remainder of the cider which had turned lukewarm. "Solon thought he had a year or more when we left Tharis. It could come at any time."

Maybe it had.

Jola still didn't know how she'd gathered the power and sent it into the earth.

Or who'd noticed. Felix hadn't mentioned anything, seeming preoccupied with Solon's role in starting the near-accident. Heron, Jola wasn't so sure of, but they were known to keep their counsel though they'd joined with Jola in insisting Solon go to the infirmary when they returned to the palace. Once there, Heron went in search of Amara while the healers insisted Solon stay the night.

Jola had stayed with Solon for a little while before a healer turned her out.

She'd thought Solon missed the way she'd handled the overflow of power, but the instant they were alone he grabbed her hand. She still had scrapes where his nails had pressed deep. *"The stones remember. I remember. What you did—you know? The bouquet?"*

"Yes?" She'd bent nearly double to hear, for he'd kept his voice low. Laid flat on a cot, his gaze wandered constantly from the window to the door and back.

"Don't tell. Keep secret. She doesn't like rivals. She tells us what to do and we do it, we don't think. That's for her."

"She?" Jola's back ached, so she dropped to kneel next to the bed. *"Do you mean Leta?"* who was Solon's usual compeer, *"or Amara? The Terparchon?"*

"Before. The old one." His nails dug deeper. *"I saw the note."*
"Note?"

"The one left when the poisoner fled. The man who nearly killed Idan," a retired compeer who'd slept in the infirmary recently. *"It was in her handwriting. She's dead. I saw her body. But she haunts us still. Don't let her know what you can do. Don't tell anyone, or she'll hear."*

Fear had rolled off him so thick she nearly gagged on the sour stench. Jola had only heard about the unravelling of the poisoner's plot after-the-fact. Nefeli shared the details, but hadn't mentioned any resemblance to her grandmother's handwriting.

Then again, Nefeli protected and guided Jola in the Dance and sometimes took that to be her role outside.

Jola shivered, returning to the moment with Nefeli's gentle fingers stroking her hand in place of Solon's hard grip.

Yet a hint of Solon's concern chilled her bones. The old Terparchon lingered indeed. Solon spoke more truth than he might realize, for Nefeli had let slip enough over the years for Jola to have some idea how much the current Terparchon still acted in defiance of her mother as though daring the previous ruler to return and challenge her.

"Solon's Danced twice your years." Nefeli shifted to sit on the couch next to Jola, body warm against hers as the packed-straw beneath them rustled under the double weight.

"The greatest difference I see between us is that I've Danced mostly with you, while he has partnered with taught compeers." Jola caressed Nefeli's cheek, rejoicing in the contact. "That's quite a difference. It's much easier with you."

"There are too few born compeers." Nefeli leaned into the caress.

"And you do not last any longer than princesses. The taught are injured more often than the born, but still . . ." Jola rose and paced the room, energy flowing through her to the point every muscle twitched. "There must be something we can do to change."

"If you can find it, all will praise your name. I remember my grandmother cursing at the speed with which she went through princesses." Nefeli returned to her couch and drained her mug.

"If there were more of us to share the load. Or a small core who traveled with the court while others remained in the various cities or regions, and had seasons to rest . . . But nothing will be done soon." Jola shook twice, then reclined back on her couch and tried to ignore her twitching toes. There had to be something, but she didn't need to persuade Nefeli or trouble her with possibilities. Hard plans were needed, and night not the best time for Jola to ponder them. She required distraction. "What of you, how was your day?"

Her lover winced. "I saw Ylena."

"How is she?" Jola half-closed her eyes, reflecting on the schedule she'd set up for princesses and compeers to visit the injured princess. She was up to visit herself in a day or two.

"Healing. The healers have her walking some, though she won't be ready when the court leaves. She'll have to remain here or ride in a cart."

Jola shuddered, muscles aching at the memory of taking a brief rest in a cart when her legs tired. That only happened at the start of the court's progress from winter palace to summer or the reverse, and then only when she didn't take care to pace herself. The oxen pulling the carts lumbered, and the wheels jolted over every stone and into every hole or puddle possible. "Is risking her leg in the carts wise?"

"Probably not." Nefeli crunched on a piece of melon. "It's a pity she's not from near enough to go home without riding far in a cart. Idan's heading up to his family tomorrow."

Jola smiled, as they both like the oldest of the born compeers. But her toes twitched again, for Idan had recently retired due to ill-health only to have it turn out to be poison.

So many strange happenings these past weeks—she'd be glad to be off and away on the long route home.

"Do you have any more dance exhibitions?" Nefeli asked.

"Today was the last. Time to start packing, the sooner we do the sooner we can leave and head home." Jola gazed up at the shadowy ceiling, imagining the return and the fuss her mothers and other family always made when she walked down the lane from the city to the rambling house on the outskirts.

"Home?"

"Tharis. My mothers' house. See my siblings and how many more children they have now. Play with them. Count the birds in the coops. Little things." Jola wouldn't make it there for another season, as the court wandered through other cities before returning to the winter palace.

"Your family's hardly a little thing."

"True, there are many of us." Jola echoed Nefeli's chuckle. Not only had her three mothers each born several children, two opened the house to care for other families' children by day or night as needed, and took in fosterlings. Over the years many strangers had become kin in all-but blood.

"You miss them."

"Very much." Jola nearly missed the odd note in Nefeli's voice, then sat up and faced her. "It's always good to get away—there's rarely a chance for peace and talking with any one for very long alone when I'm there—but the longer I'm away the more I want to see them again."

"We'll leave soon." Nefeli bent over and wrapped her arms around Jola. "You'll be there before you know it."

Jola managed a smile and leaned into Nefeli's embrace, but her lover didn't understand. As a member of the royal family, she'd grown up with the cycle of moving between cities. She'd never had one home where nearly all her loved ones remained, where all her childhood memories centered.

Being in Nefeli's arms was also home for Jola, but a different kind. For all that Jola chose it and would do so again, she missed her family.

5

Nefeli left her warm bed and traipsed across the royal wing to a small chamber she'd never before visited.

The door closed behind her with an unexpectedly heavy thud. She jerked, for most of the doors in the royal wing of the palace moved silently and clicked into place. The legions of servants kept the hinges well-oiled.

Save this, evidently.

She leaned back against the smooth wood as the cool late-summer dawn leached warmth from her. Bumps formed along her arms and legs despite the protective layers of her calf-length gold tunic and red mantle. She'd dressed for the day, but her circlet seemed to have turned into a band of ice rather than entwined strands of gold and copper. The metal pinned her short, black curls against the sides of her head.

Indeed, every bit of jewelry on her body absorbed some of the chill, from the slender gold bangles at her wrists, only a few shades less ruddy than her skin to the chain belted around her waist to the matching bangles at her ankles. The anklets hung over the straps binding her leather sandals to her feet. Just as well to give her a hint of protection against the no-doubt cool stone floor. Nevertheless, tremors rippled through her calves and set the anklets chiming. Instead of their usual delicate peal—a mellow tone meant to reassure people she wasn't sneaking up on them merely because she happened to walk lighter than they expected a short, solid-built person to do— the anklets clashed. The sound assaulted her ears to the point she was tempted to remove them,

For the first time since coming to the summer palace, she was truly cool.

Nevertheless, the almost-still air carried the moist scent of the morning dew beginning to burn off mixed with a hint of sweat.

Not hers.

This wasn't a room she'd ever visited before. The narrow chamber had little to recommend it. Walls, floor, and ceiling all lacked any decoration whatsoever—no mosaic or painting. The plaster showed brushmarks from a recent coat of white-wash, and the stone floor was clean. That was about all it had to recommend itself.

The furnishings were similarly simple. A narrow bed stretched the length of the wall to her right, covered by a wrinkled light blue and white blanket that had seen better days given the number of times it had been patched.

Two doors, both closed, comprised most of the matching wall to the left.

The opposite wall had windows offering a view of a narrow courtyard good for little more than getting from the palace proper to the dancing pavilion. She peered this way and that, but at best the windows boasted only the merest sliver of a lake view.

A plain table-desk with matching chair rested where a sitter might make the most of that view. The table was bare, but a couple of volumes bound in red and gold sat on a shelf above the bed.

The room lacked clothes press or piles of clothes on the remainder of the single shelf.

Yet someone had slept in the bed recently. Given who had asked her to come here, unattended, at this early hour, Nefeli could guess who even without her gift.

With it, she knew. The subtle magic that flowed through her veins, as a born compeer, let her track people. The better to partner princesses in the Dance, that was all the value most people assigned to her. Few cared to wonder what else born compeers might do. Nefeli could count on the fingers of her hands how many people appreciated the complexities. At most, they recognized her ability to know who lingered near her at any time, a power she usually limited to her immediate environs. But compeers' abilities extended to discover where people were—and where they'd passed.

Only one person had lingered here based on the testimony of the stone floor. Stones didn't speak, but surfaces understood who passed over them.

Her father slept here, and more than once.

It made no sense. He had plenty of other beds available. He was the Marchon, second only to the Terparchon in importance. The royal suite included a large bedroom for him with an excellent lake view, placed right next to her mother's matching bedchamber should they not share a bed. She tried not to track her parents' bedroom habits. Still, although Nefeli had never heard rumors of him seeking comfort with people other than her mother, there were many among the court who would welcome him should he choose.

Yet he'd evidently settled on this small chamber. A room she didn't remember ever being in before, or even being aware existed, despite having roamed the whole of the royal wing in her younger years.

Then again, she'd stopped routinely tracking him and her mother when they first started plotting to overthrow her grandmother. Although barely in her teens at the time, Nefeli had feared letting anything accidentally let slip to the old Terparchon, a woman Nefeli never doubted her parents were were right to fear. She'd never returned to doing so after.

She generally restricted herself to checking on them once per season unless explicitly asked to find them, and even then only when given permission to do so—which they gave, as did everyone she'd asked. Strange that still, no matter often or how many varied ways she tried to explain what she was and could do, only other born compeers ever truly understood.

Still, she should have known of the existence of this out-of-reach room—and the chance that her father would use it for sleeping before he asked her to rise from her comfortable bed early in the morning. A sacrifice, too, for she'd had to leave the warm body of her lover behind, slumbering in her bed, to come meet him.

Before she could wonder if she'd come to the wrong place, footfalls down the hall reverberated in her bones. Each bore certainty as to who approached, that he came alone, and a hint of his mood: pensive.

The near door opened with a creak and her father slipped through. He eased the door shut behind him, with a click rather than a thud.

Furrows marked his brow, as his skin was the color of parchment with a tendency to show lines where it wasn't stretched over muscles that attested to the hours he spent working with the guards. Warm brown eyes touched with tiredness looked out from beneath short, bright brown hair only starting to grizzle. Thin lips were pulled almost straight, inclining down at the ends, under a steep nose. She'd gotten her solidity and strength from him, along with his nose and eyes.

She'd also inherited or picked up from him a preference for yellows, oranges, and reds in attire. Although she hadn't consulted him on her clothing nor, so far as she knew, either of their servants, they'd wound up wearing almost the exact same shades of tunic and mantle, granted his clothing fell only to his knees rather than mid-calf.

On the other hand, she'd gotten her penchant for jewelry from her mother. He wore only a light chain around one ankle. His bare feet padded across the floor. He carried a light cream platter edged in gilt that bore two fresh-baked redberry pastries—her favorite and his.

Her stomach rumbled as the sweet, honeyed scent filled the air.

"One for you, one for me." He smiled as he held out the platter.

She grabbed one and nearly dropped it in surprise at the warmth. Truly fresh from the oven, cooled just enough to eat.

Glorious flavor filled her mouth, sweet with a hint of sour. So easy to consume. Bite followed bite, for every moment leached a little more warmth from the pastry and it was best when hot.

Best gobbled down with hardly a pause.

Hardly royal behavior, and not something she ever did in front of anyone except her father—and Jola.

The privacy of the small chamber gave her the freedom to finishes it off fast, though no faster than her father. The platter lay abandoned on the table as they licked the last drops of honey from their fingers.

Nefeli stretched, lifting her arms high overhead, as the pastry's warmth spiraled out from her belly to flow through every part of her body. A hint of chill followed, for the pastries alone could not explain his request for the early morning visit, or his choice of this out-of-the way room where they would not be overheard.

"Wonderful."

"The cooks elsewhere try, but there's nothing to match these." Her father rubbed his belly.

"Even Rorenber?" The city her father had grown up in was known for glorious baking.

He froze, eyes wide. After a moment, his lips curved to one side. He pressed a finger against them, gaze sad. "Don't tell."

"Promise." She touched her own lips, then waved at the chamber. "Yet why indulge now, here."

He leaned back against table. The wood groaned under his weight, or was he gripping the edge? She couldn't tell without making it obvious she checked. Then again, did she need to? His shoulders slumped and the number of lines on his face increased.

Tiredness seeped from his soles into the floor. Enough filtered through to her that she nearly yawned from his need. He had to know she'd notice, though she often struggled to discern what information about themselves people sought to keep secret and didn't realize they'd betrayed in ways born compeers might read.

His exhaustion was real. She believed it. Still, that didn't mean he wasn't using it to prolong their meeting—to put off whatever he had to say. He'd often met her for pastries in the past, just as he did with her brother and sister, but at least half the time the sweet served as prelude to bad news.

He was the one who'd comforted her over the years. And warned her in advance of meetings with her mother, of which this had all the hallmarks.

"What, is it the first pass in convincing me to do something?" Nefeli retreated until she had the cool stone wall at her back.

He almost smiled at that, though he didn't affirm or deny. He did, at least, break silence. "Leading citizens of Erevestis will visit Yaras in a few weeks."

"Everyone's heard that by now."

"Does everyone know they'll arrive after the court departs?" He asked.

"No." The pastry suddenly sat heavier in her belly.

"To be more precise, approximately two-thirds of the court will leave before they visit. There are too many visits to other cities planned, and meetings already set with those who rule the different parts of Codaros in your mother's name—"

"And yours." She jerked her chin at him, staring into his eyes.

"And mine." He tilted his head to the side and matched her gaze. "But someone must be here to welcome the Erevestisi, to render back the honor they do us by visiting—and show them around, most especially the former Shadow of the Moon."

"Wretched things." She shivered and glanced away. Every time Nefeli had visited the various Shadows of the Moon scattered, her skin itched and she longed to be anywhere else. The uncanny sites were perfect, round beds of white rock slowly growing and consuming the earth around them. Each of the cities in Codaros boasted one, as did another handful of cities outside . . . except Yaras. In the span of a single night earlier in the summer, the local Shadow had vanished. Hit by lightning, and somehow replaced with strange flowers. "I wouldn't mind if lightning struck them all."

His chest heaved, although only a slight huff of a chuckle escaped his lips. "No delegations from Erevestis have visited in over a decade. All negotiations are held through other cities, and whenever citizens of Codaros visit there they are carefully watched."

"So we're to host the Erevestisi now that they're willing to visit, and see what information, and concessions, we can extract from them in return?"

"Yes"

Nefeli twitched, arms pulling in again her side. His blunt honesty only added to the sinking sensation in her stomach, for he usually danced around the sordid realities of governing.

"It's not a task for your mother. If she stays behind, rather than leaves for the usual visits, we risk much. There are those who will deal with none but her, and will take offense should she send another in her place."

"You?" She waved a hand at him.

"The same may be said of me, to a degree." He patted his chest. "I, too, have too many places I must be before the court reunites in Tharis. No, we need an acceptable deputy. Or two."

True enough. Codaros was a patchwork land, formed by a mix of aggressive Terparchons eager to conquer and expand its boundaries and those Terparchons who favored the slow labor of building ties between the uneasy cities connected by wars. So many people wanting so many different things, with never an easy answer to any question.

This least of all.

She waited, watching him. He lifted an eyebrow at her and understanding dawned.

"Mother wants me to act as host?" One foot twitched, setting her anklets chiming. She'd stood in for one or both of her parents before, the first time when she was young enough she remembered little more than being wrapped in stiff clothes and enough jewelry that made movement difficult while towering adults went to their knees before her. "Does she know you're telling me this?"

"She knows enough." This time he turned away, walking over to the bed. It creaked as he sat down, hands folded in his lap.

"Why are you warning me." Hosting a delegation hardly ranked as warranting advance warning except that it gave Nefeli an opportunity to decide what concessions she might want from her mother in return for her willing consent. "Do you think I'm fool enough to say no if she asks me in public?"

"She won't, not at first." He glanced at her, then away.

"What do I need to know?" Nefeli's voice dropped. She swallowed the sudden lump that turned her tones to scarce more than a whisper, but it reformed.

"She'll leave you a couple of princesses, along with appropriate courtiers, servants, and guards."

He failed to mention that Nefeli's mother would certainly leave her compeers to partner the princesses. He was a taught compeer rather than a born one, but still he'd Danced in that capacity, partnering the Terparchon, since before Nefeli was born. Alas, as with so many others, he failed to appreciate the value compeers brought to the Dance.

Likewise, he might not realize that he leaked unease. Nefeli shifted her stance, tapping each foot against the floor before replacing it. The movement reduced the extent to which his discomfort affected her. Unfortunately, she'd already caught it from him. The warming airs of mornings slipped into through the window, but Nefeli's bones remained chilled.

Taking a deep breath, he sat straight. He lifted his chin. Stared at her. "You will have the opportunity to advise her on which princesses you wish to remain."

The leap left Nefeli's mouth gaping. She snapped it shut as she puzzled through his words. Advise on who she wanted left with her? There were only twelve active princesses, and matching compeers, with her mother and father dancing as the thirteenth.

Twelve divided into three quite nicely, unless her mother preferred unequal numbers since four wasn't good for Dancing. Prime numbers were best, so likely a three and two groups of five. Which meant if Nefeli ended up being part of the three, she'd encourage her mother to assign two of the more powerful princesses and compeers to remain.

Yet he'd said only princesses, not princesses and compeers. Likely his usual way of forgetting that compeers mattered—or had he emphasized the word princesses?

For Nefeli was a compeer. If she were remaining to host the delegation, she'd needed one more princess than compeer. Her choice would lead the princesses, and welcome the envoys beside her.

Of course she'd chose Jola.

Or did her father—or mother—have any concerns over that?

"What are you not telling me?"

The bed squeaked again as her father rose and approached her. He stopped a few hands away, close enough for her to smell the redberries on his breath and shiver at the chill pouring off his bones.

"Keep this next quiet and close—it's my guess only." He held out his palm.

"On my honor." She slapped his hand, jerking as a rill of power rippled through her. He so rarely asked for full secrecy.

"One of the most crucial tests of any ruler lies before your mother." His voice dropped although no one was anywhere close enough to hear.

Then again, as a taught compeer he lacked the power to be sure.

"And that is?" She leaned in.

"The choice of successor."

Every hair on Nefeli's body stiffened. Her arms and legs shook, slight movements but enough to raise a low hum of chimes from her bracelets and anklets.

"I thought she had decided."

The Terparchon had alluded to the matter on a number of occasions, albeit without ever naming names, but also without showing a thread of doubt. Most of the rumors in the court whispered she'd chosen Todor and Ylena. Nefeli had even heard speculation to that effect from her sister.

Yet every time Nefeli had heard her mother refer to the issue of heirs it was in terms open to more than one interpretation. For her part, she'd guessed her mother favored Zora who mostly met the necessary requirements—even though Zora had been the favorite of their grandmother.

Was the request for Nefeli to host the envoys a hint of a different plan?

"Me?" She pressed her hands against the wall. Refused to sway, despite the rush of blood away from her head.

"You're the oldest."

"That makes no difference, as all of mother's siblings would attest." Nefeli swallowed, glaring at him. "How many older were still alive when grandmother named her as heir?"

He nodded, face soft with sympathy. "You're the oldest daughter."

"Mother had an older sister." Granted, she'd died under questionable circumstances shortly after Nefeli's parents' married.

"This will be your mother's choice." The Marchon traced her cheek with a warm but shaky finger. "I can only advise, and even that only as far as she's willing to listen. Since neither you nor your siblings are princesses, I thought she might select your brother, since he seemed matched with a capable and ambitious princess."

An understatement. Ylena was one of the most powerful and purposeful princesses Nefeli'd ever met, even felled by the broken leg.

"But now I think otherwise." Nefeli's father set his hands on her shoulders. "Be warned, as she may make you the offer at the same time as she asks you to serve as host."

Nefeli needed his hands bracing her.

She'd wondered whether she might one day rule, no matter that her parents recognized early that compeer magic bloomed in her veins rather than princess. Especially after the births of her younger siblings, neither seeming blessed with magic.

Except every time she saw her grandmother, the former Terparchon, the older woman pinched Nefeli's cheek and leaned in close to remind her to remember her place for "princesses rule, compeers serve."

Half the time, she'd turn and beam at Zora. "I'll make a princess of you yet," she'd pat the younger girl's head.

Though Zora rarely showed any sign she wanted the throne in her own right.

Nefeli's mother might give her elder daughter a chance to turn things upside down, to rule hand-in-hand with a princess.

There was the catch. Which?

Jola surely. Her parents knew Nefeli and Jola were lovers. Everyone at court understood, although the two had not yet sworn binding vows.

But they'd kept company several years, long enough for Nefeli to know that Jola showed little desire to rule, though much interest in what rules were made and how they were carried out. She'd be an asset to any ruler with her connections in every part of the land through her dance exchange program, though Nefeli valued her for so many other reasons as well.

Her father had welcomed Jola as Nefeli's chosen companion from the first, even before the Terparchon.

Still, he'd chosen to warn Nefeli of the upcoming change alone. Without Jola.

"Do I have the right to choose with whom I Dance?" In short, decide who would be Terparchon to her Marchon should she stand as her parents' heir. The words scraped her throat as they emerged, low and hoarse.

"Perhaps." He wrapped his arms around her, and she fell into his hug glad he couldn't see her face. Burying her head against his chest didn't prevent his words from echoing in her ears. "But your time to choose is coming to an end. Consider your remaining behind to host the Erevestisi as a test of you and your preferred princess, whomever they may be."

How could Nefeli put Jola through this unless she was willing . . . what if she wasn't? Or fell pray to nerves and failed? Or . . .

Regardless of whether Jola was willing to become Terparchon, Nefeli staying to host the envoys meant asking her lover to put off leaving the summer palace immediately after Jola had expressed a longing to be off on her way to Tharis, which she still considered home.

Jola could refuse the request, but if Ylena were right she wouldn't want to deny Nefeli.

And Nefeli would do as her parents wished. Her father's unofficial warning gave her a chance to pull backbit she wouldn't. If her mother offered her the right of succession, she'd take it—surely with Jola at her side?

6

Jola often left Nefeli's rooms soon after her lover. They were always empty on her own.

Then again, so were her own rooms. She leaned back against the wooden door and surveyed the tidy array. No dust gathered on the floor, but wood planks had a dull appearance all the same save where covered by a thin, braided circular rug in yellows and oranges. When Jola moved forward, she could almost see the marks from her sandals.

She wore no jewelry, and only a plain unbleached tunic and simple yellow mantle, for she was ready to work.

Fortunately, she'd chosen a single chamber rather than the two-room suites most princesses enjoyed. After all, she spent most of her time in Nefeli's rooms, though Jola preferred to keep her things in her own.

The air in the room was cool thanks to the closed shutters, but also musty. Or, rather, there was an air of disuse. The cover on the bed in the corner had hardly a wrinkle. Likewise, the couch for visitors to lounge on boasted plump cushions rarely weighted down by anyone. Only the shelving along the interior wall saw much use, holding piles of clean tunics, mantles, and sandals.

The floor boards didn't creak under her as she crossed to open the shutters and let in the morning air. It was warmer outside—this was about the time of day most people closed their shutters against the heat—but she wanted it.

She was cold, but not just because of the relative cool of the lat summer morning.

Usually Jola woke before Nefeli, summer and winter. After years of rising early to do chores, Jola never managed to completely shake off the habit and adjust to later days.

Besides, that gave her time to admire her lover. Nefeli alternately sprawled across two-thirds of the bed and cuddled up close to Jola—a picture either way.

Plus, rising early allowed Jola to slip discreetly out, back to her own rooms, while most of the palace was still waking. She did so mostly to swap out clothes as she preferred not to keep more than a few pieces of attire in Nefeli's suite. Their rooms were close enough to each other, after all. Jola only had to creep down a hall and over a bridge connecting the princesses' wing with the royal residence.

She could make it without anyone noticing, when she tried.

Their affair was not a secret. Everyone who cared in the court, and some who didn't surely knew, but the quieter Jola kept the liaison on her part the easier a time she'd have when it ended. Not easy, but easier.

And it would be over someday, even though that day keeps moving farther and farther down the road.

But maybe it no longer sat far away anymore—because this morning, Nefeli woke first. Woke, rose, and left without Jola noticing.

When she did shake sleep from her eyes, she was alone in the bed and cold despite the covers.

So she returned to her room.

Her stomach rumbled. Could be hunger, or could be nausea.

Jola checked the pitcher sitting in a bowl on the table near the sofa. Emmi, the servant who oversaw Jola's care and that of a few other princesses, had filled it the day before. The water remained fresh enough, albeit lukewarm. Jola drank until her stomach eased.

An hour or more remained before the bell would ring for daily dance practice. That wouldn't last long, just enough to keep them all limber and ready. It was late enough in the summer that the worst of the storms are done. Autumn storms rarely threatened the shore to the extent of the summer.

The court would leave the summer palace soon. Which at least gave her something to do rather than ponder Nefeli's strange early morning abandonment of their bed.

Jola set herself to sorting her belongings into those items to pack and take with her versus those to store in a trunk that would remain behind in the palace for the next year.

Some princesses, compeers, and courtiers made the divisions but left the details to their servants. Others trusted servants to make most or all decisions.

Jola preferred to do the sorting and packing herself. Partly because she didn't grow up with servants and still hadn't completely adjusted to having them do things for her, but also because the one time she had stepped back—after her first season at the summer palace—a few things she'd wanted had been left behind.

Most particularly a small leather bag holding a glass lens that Jola used see things far away. It didn't work as well as it had when she was younger, but she still treasured it. Her mothers hadn't ever said just how much they'd given up to get it for her.

It had gone missing by the time they returned the next summer.

Nefeli tracked it down for her. Jola still didn't know why the eldest daughter of the Terparchon took note of the loss at the time. Granted, Nefeli had been young enough then to not yet serve as a compeer although everyone knew she'd one day be one. She was still finishing up her schooling in the children's palace yet she'd headed off into the city and returned with the lens and bag in almost the same condition as they'd been when lost.

That was the official start of their friendship, although Jola had admired Nefeli for much longer. Neither realized they'd become more, though they didn't kiss until two years later.

Starting at the far end, Jola sorted her clothes into piles on the bed and sofa. These could be left in trunks in storage, that packed in the carts that wouldn't be unloaded often, another set for stops along the way, and the smallest for the remaining days before the court departed. Her hands kept busy checking soft lengths of cloth for stains and fraying hems.

Yet she kept putting items in the wrong pile.

Maybe Jola could hold onto her friendship with Nefeli, even if it had to change, to dwindle. Which it did, for Nefeli was royal and the oldest child of the Terparchon. The oldest daughter.

And Jola?

From a rambling house at the edge of Tharis overflowing with children. She could go back, when she stops being a princess. Another pair of hands was always welcome.

Or she might become a musician or take a place at court supporting other princesses and compeers. Only former princesses and compeers are allowed in the chambers where the current Dance.

Alternatively, she might teach dancing, or a host of other possibilities.

But she wasn't ready, not yet.

Always hoped that Nefeli wouldn't tire of Jola until she was on the point of retiring. It would double the hurt, losing place and love at the same time, but let her go free on to whatever else.

If she didn't burn out first.

Was Solon right about what's going on with Jola something she shouldn't share? He'd been so cryptic, yet his fear had slipped into her. She could still hear his hoarse words of warning.

Yet surely Jola could ask Amara, the oldest of the retired princesses remaining with the court.

Or Nefeli.

Except what if it was a sign Jola risked burning out or doing something worse?

Pacing brought her to the point where she can see through the window to the gardens in the distance. It was mostly a blur, but she didn't have to make out details to know what the view included: the clearing in the middle of the gardens where the Shadow of the Moon once was. A circle of unusual flowers grew there instead. Beautiful to look at, and giving off an aroma that eased cares. For a moment, Jola caught a hint of it in the air.

Except the tang increased her desire to go far away. Everyone at court and in the city knew a strange bolt of lightning destroyed the Shadow and replaced it with flowers. Many doubted.

Only a few know how and why it happened.

Was that what started the change in Jola toward burnout or danger?

So many worries. She'd promised not to tell about the lightning and how it happened. Now that secret had another: whatever she'd done during the dance with Solon.

Surely she could tell Nefeli.

Unless that changed things between them.

Dropping a luscious orange mantle, she rapped her head. The brief flash of pain made her start, despite being expected.

Silly to go fretting over something that hadn't happened and might not. Part of the joy of being a princess was the ability to Dance and change or lessen dangers.

She should take a lesson from that. Nothing was set until it happened.

She could at least ask Nefeli if it was time for their affair to end, instead of assuming.

What if she were right?

Then she'd know.

And could go make plans based on that.

For she might not be right. Maybe this wasn't the first sign of Nefeli turning away.

Except, what if Jola asking tilted the scales towards them parting?

Her head ached, and not from the rap. If only she were more like Heron or Solon or Danissa, all princesses who always seemed so much more self-assured.

"You're a princess, so be one" Danissa had told Jola more than once, even though the younger woman hadn't become a princess until years after Jola. "Why are you always so deferential? You've earned your place, your honor."

Easy for Danissa to say when she'd grown up at court with a father who was the longest serving of the compeers. If she hadn't played as a child with Nefeli, she had with Todor or Zora.

Versus growing up far from court.

Jola had learned to speak up, to stand forward, to act. How else would she have managed to start the dance programs in the summer and winter capitals? But it was all a facade. Underneath she was still the stunned young woman—girl, really—reft from her home with little warning to Dance with princesses.

How many years had she spent here not feeling as though she fully belonged?

Would she ever?

She leapt, clutching a pile of tunics to her chest, at a sudden knock on the door.

Who would come, when nearly everyone knew she rarely spent time here? Most likely one or another of the servants, come to help pack in advance of the move.

Yet little surprise trickled through Jola when she opened to end Nefeli on the other side. The other woman also wore a simple tunic and mantle, but several bracelets and anklets that chimed as she shifted her weight from foot to foot.

Something loosened in Jola and she smiled, because the presence, the mere sight, of Nefeli made her more at ease no matter her worries.

Except when Nefeli showed discomfort.

Jola's smile flickered, slipped. She stood aside so her lover could enter.

In a contrast to the night before, Nefeli paced around the room barely glancing at it. She hadn't been here often, but likely noted every change and every bit of clothing sorted or unsorted.

"You're packing."

"Of course I am. There's barely time until we leave." Jola shut the door and leaned back against it again, lacing her fingers together. "We're in your father's train again this time, right?" The Terparchon and Marchon split the court and took different routes, to give every part of the country more opportunities to see—and be seen—by one or the other.

And route was warmer and drier than the other, so it does make a bit of a difference on what to pack. Each took half the princesses and compeers with them and the assignments were usually made well in advance, but the Terparchon sometimes changed which princesses and compeers went with whom.

"Are you so anxious to go?" Nefeli asked, whirling around to face Jola.

"Oh, yes." The wealth of the summer's happenings gave Jola ample reason to want to be away—the loss of Ylena to injury, the new princess, the destruction of the Shadow of the Moon, and the strange dance with Solon and Heron. Without explaining any of it, she offered the easiest and simplest answer that was also true. "I miss home."

Nefeli dropped onto the bed, perching atop a pile of tunics and mantles. Her hands gripped the sides of her mantle tight, knuckles gray. "Would it be so hard to stay?"

"Stay where?"

"Here." Nefeli let go of her mantle and opened her hands.

Jola's head lurched back, hitting the door. She stumbled forward. Pushing a pile of mantles aside, she sat on the couch only an arm's length from Nefeli. Shivering, she grabbed a mantle at random and wrapped it around her shoulders. "Alone?"

"No!" Leaping from bed to couch, Nefeli wrapped her arms around Jola. "Never alone."

Under any other circumstances, Jola would tuck her head against Nefeli's neck. She remained hunched over instead, shoulders up around her ears. "With you?" Her voice cracked, and she turned her face away.

"That's the idea." Nefeli hugged Jola tight, rocking her. "I'm doing this badly. I'm sorry, I don't . . . This is for your ears only, until it is announced."

Swallowing hard, Jola forced down the lump in her throat. She risked a glance over her shoulder and noted the grayish cast to Nefeli's face. Whatever it was, it had shaken her. Jola shifted and let the mantle slip from her shoulders as she returned Nefeli's embrace. "Promise."

Jola's lover drew in a huge breath, arms remaining tight around Jola. Then she eased her hold and pulled back just far enough for them to gaze into each other's eyes. Rays of warm yellow sunlight slipped in through the open window, raising sweat on their brows but they remained in place regardless.

"Some of the court, as much as a third, will stay behind, to host the Erevestisi envoys."

Jola blinked. She'd heard rumors of the envoys but not teased out ramifications. Supposedly news of the former Shadow-turned-flowers had prompted the other land to end their silence and reach out.

So they'd come, and the court or part would remain to greet them. A dozen different questions rushed through Jola, or rather a dozen ways to ask the same question: what did that mean for the two of them?

Rather than spill too much and ask the wrong way, she waited. Gritted her teeth. Set her feet flat on the floor, kicking out of the way a tunic that had fallen from the bed.

There were too many possibilities. Better to wait and let Nefeli choose what to share versus pushing.

"You understand?" Nefeli's brow wrinkled and she studied Jola close.

"Someone has to host the envoys, but . . . not the whole court?" Jola asked.

"No. One third will continue on the southern route, as planned, and the other on the northern. The last will remain here." Nefeli clasped Jola's right hand between hers. "Where do you want to be?"

"With you." Jola placed her left hand outside Nefeli's, so that they both clasped and were clasped.

"It can't be just that." Nefeli's fingers were cold against Jola's skin.

"What do you mean?"

"Being with me means . . . More will be required of you. Say I remain behind, to host the envoys in my parents' stead."

Jola blinked and squinted. Of course Nefeli would be needed in some official capacity. She'd be an excellent choice for host: even-tempered, diplomatic, and immovable unless she so chose. Even if Ylena wasn't injured and were able to stand beside Todor, Jola considered Nefeli the better option. "Is that what you're going to do?"

"I'll need princesses and compeers with me." Nefeli's hold tightened. "Only a few, those that can be spared from my parent's trains. Together we'll represent my parents and ensure the envoys don't take offense or advantage."

Jola licked her lips and drew in a deep breath. "What do you need of me?"

"I need a partner in all ways. One able to adjust however the waves of fate carry us—whether that be low or high."

"I will follow you wherever you go." Already Jola's lips were dry again. Her whole body turned stiff, the world seeming distant other than Nefeli. Only their clasped hands were real.

"Even if it means staying with me, here, when you long for home."

"Yes."

"Even if it requires that you lead, rather than follow?"

"I don't . . . Lead?" Jola's voice squeaked on the last word. She'd led many a dance exhibition over the years, ordering princesses and compeers around left and right. Yet never in magic, only in powerless movement.

Save that last accidental Dance when Solon had lost control.

"Princesses lead in the dance, compeers follow." Nefeli leaned closer, dark eyes intent on Jola. "My mother leads, my father follows."

"You know it's not that simple. You and the other born compeers do much more." The protest escaped Jola without thought.

"We know, but others do not." Nefeli shrugged the general disregard for compeers off as she always did. Her hands tightened around Jola's, then she let go and sat back. "Are you willing to lead and be seen to lead?"

"What are you asking?" Jola stood and walked to the window, hands trembling as she closed the shutters. Shadows filled the room. Her eyes required time to adjust, but she didn't have to strain. Nefeli, too, rose. The other woman remained just out of reach.

"You're known to be my partner, in bed but also in the Dance. If you stay with me, to host the envoys, it will be a statement. You will share the duties and be host as much as I." Nefeli extended her hand.

Jola stared at it, realizing some part of what's her lover wanted of her: to be a stand-in for the Terparchon. Yet Nefeli didn't command, she asked. She offered a simple choice.

Stand at her side . . . or not.

$\mathbf{\$}$ 7 $\mathbf{\%}$

Nefeli's forearm ached as she kept her hand extended. Time slowed so that she lost track of how much had passed, how long she'd waited.

Her head ached with pleas, words that longed to spill from her mouth. She locked her jaw and prisoned them inside. Best to let none escape lest she influence Jola's decision.

Of all places, why did they stand in Jola's room. Jola hardly needed the narrow space. A single chamber mingling entertaining and sleeping together. The bed set against one wall might hold two only if they squeezed. One couch for lounging rather than two, meaning they either shared or one reclined on the bed. Yet most of Jola's clothes adorned the shelves in neatly folded piles, or hung from pegs along the wall. A faint preservative scent cloyed the air, no doubt intended to keep nibbling insects away but much more acrid than whatever was used in Nefeli's quarters.

Given a choice, Nefeli would have swept Jola and her belongings into her larger rooms. Surely the fact that Jola maintained her separate place showed she made her own decisions rather than letting Nefeli make them for her.

Jola hesitated, hand partly extended. The delicate flutters of her fingers raised a small breeze caressing Nefeli's skin. Eyes big in the half-light, the princess resembled a bird readying to fly away—and this only at the offer to stand in for the Terparchon when hosting the envoys.

Then again, Nefeli's belly roiled and her mouth was dry. If she could tremble she would, but that would help nothing. She wanted time to sit and consider all the implications of the impending offer from her mother. But before Nefeli had tracked Jola down, a messenger had brought word from her mother.

A time and a place—that night, before dinner.

Nefeli wanted Jola with her, especially if she was named heir.

She shouldn't have closed the light baskets. Darkness offered the intimacy and closeness of night when they lay together in Nefeli's big bed. The half-open baskets combined with sunlight creeping through cracks in the shutters to create dimness instead. Lines of shadow crossed Jola's face. Nefeli couldn't see well enough to note any subtleties of expression.

How many times had Nefeli unthinkingly chosen shadows when she knew Jola didn't see well at distances? But she did close up. And she could have protested any time.

Nefeli's brain churned and her skin grew cold. This wasn't like her. She didn't waver back and forth examining a million possibilities—she chose her ground and stayed there. She was the rock, the support for when Jola danced.

Yet Ylena's poisonous comparison ate at Nefeli. Slipped in everywhere, recasting choice after choice. She had to wait, let Jola decide on her own.

A sour taste bloomed in her mouth.

Her hand shook--right as Jola grasped it. Their chilled fingers twined. Nefeli brought up her other hand to wrap around Jola's.

"Tell me more."

"About?" Nefeli squinted through the dimness. Her lover had taken her hand, did that not mean she'd agreed?

"What you expect, what will happen, what you need."

"Ah, well." Nefeli guided Jole over to sit on the couch. The seat matched those in her rooms for comfort, although rather firmer. The scent of the straw used to stuff it permeated the air. The time "This is all unofficial. My father brought word, but I haven't talked to my mother yet. That's tonight."

"His word isn't official?"

"Not for this. My mother has the final say on who takes power. Also, it was just the two of us. No one else knows. If he is right, then she'll ask me to be host in her place and only after I accept will she announce it openly. After that there'll be no turning back. He wanted to give me warning, before she asks. Since I'm not a princess, I'll be standing in my father's place and she'll want me to name who'll partner with me."

Her jaw snapped shut. Relief at having shared details warred with thin ripples of all-but pain that snaked along her arms and legs. She hadn't mentioned the possibility that this would lead to being named heirs to the Terparchon and Marchon. She couldn't. The words of her promise to her father bound her.

Jola pulled back, head tilting to the side as she studied Nefeli.

Nefeli drew a deep breath and adjusted her seat so that one of the slanted beams of sunlight through the shutters fell across her face. Her cheeks heated and nose itched.

"They know it will be me?" Jola asked.

"They know I'm asking you. My father does, at least, and surely my mother as well. Who else would I go to first and always?" Nefeli swallowed and rubbed her dry lips. "There are options, if you'd rather not . . . though, that would raise questions and whispers and rumors. Even if we were to say that it was your choice, not everyone would believe it. Some might think I'm turning away. Or worse."

"There will be talk either way." A chuckle escaped Jola, and her fingers warmed within Nefeli's clasp. "I've been at court long enough to know that. But . . ." She leaned in, gazing direct at Nefeli's eyes. "Who would you ask if not me?"

Jola's feet rested square on the floor, calf muscles trembling. Nefeli's shoulders ached, muscles tight. She gritted her teeth, resisting the urge to read any deeper. Just a little—so she could take hope from Jola's questioning.

"I don't know. Maybe Amara, even though she's retired, but possibly Ylena."

"She'd be a good choice." Jola's fingers fluttered, but she lifted her free hand so that they both held the other.

"She's not you." Nefeli tilted toward her, then pulled back as the light fell directly into her eyes and made the shadows dance for a moment.

She missed whatever expression passed across Jola's face, but recovered in time to rejoice in her lover's strong "no."

"No." Jola repeated. Her chest rose and fell with a deep breath, grip tightening. "I'm not saying no. I don't want . . . If anyone stands beside you, I want it to be me. I just . . . Need to know what it is I'm saying yes to."

"Oh." Nefeli slumped then shook, loosening the tension in her shoulders without letting go. A thin layer of sweat formed between their matched hands. The handclasp shifted, but Nefeli held on. "Well, part of court will leave with my father to visit the Southern and Eastern parts of the nation. More will go with my mother to the North. The rest—perhaps a third—will remain here. We may have to pull back and let some of the buildings be closed, as there won't be enough of us to fill the palace."

She glance pointedly around Jola's rooms. Wouldn't mind a reason for her lover to move in fully into her rooms.

"And?" Jola asked.

"We'll host the envoys. There'll be festivities of some type. Small, since we're only a slice of court, but certainly a formal reception. A meal or two with local dignitaries. A tour of the palace or parts of it, the most famous mosaics and gardens. Perhaps a ceremonial dance of some type, and of course exchanges of gifts. You know the kind of thing." Nefeli finally let go, wiping her palms on her tunic and then waving her hands in the air. "Among all that, there will be chances to talk to them, to find out more about why they've been politely ignoring us—other than allowing our traders to use their harbor and certain routes through their territory—for years. Decades. Centuries even."

"Yet they're breaking the silence to visit now."

"The letter they sent says they want to see the Shadow of the Moon."

"The one here, that doesn't exist." Jola's arms pressed tight against her side, and her voice shifted higher.

Her tension didn't surprise Nefeli. Neither particularly liked the Shadows—the rounds of deathly white stone scattered across the continent. Many didn't, though others were fascinated. The Shadow near Tharis, the winter capital, sat just outside the city and was popular with visitors. The Shadow at Yaras lay within the summer palace bounds and was rarely open for visitation while court was around.

Though that had changed slightly in the past weeks—since a great bolt of lightning had struck the Shadow and destroyed all signs of it.

"I should say rather that they want to see the flowers that appeared in its place. They are beautiful and well worth viewing." She and Jola had gone out to see the mysterious blooms a few days after their appearance, once the guards considered it safe at least at a reasonable distance.

Glorious night-blue blossoms on tall stalks had given off a sweet aroma Nefeli had only to close her eyes to remember. She'd inhaled deeply, but Jola had been uneasy even with the commander of the guards' assurance that no one had shown any sign of ill effects from being near.

"They are that." Jola shuddered, a hand slipping back into Nefeli's.

"We'll take them out, let them see their fill. Perhaps talk about trade or establishing a more formal relationship between our lands. See what we learn. Then . . ." Nefeli leaned forward, squeezing Jola's fingers and beaming at the good news she had to offer. "After they leave, we go home."

"Join the Terparchon or Marchon?"

"No, head straight for Tharis. Unless the Erevestisi stay for weeks on end, which I doubt, we'll be at the winter palace before the start of winter."

An extra benefit and reason for Jola to agree. Her eyes lit at the news, though Nefeli was glad Jola had agreed before learning the additional reason.

"That's all?" Jola raised a foot and jiggled it. "No Dancing?"

"There shouldn't be a need. The storm season is all-but over. The Erevestisi aren't sending a large party—my father assured me of that. Although, you will be advised to keep more guards around you if you venture into the city but even while wandering the palace." Additional reason for that as well, which Nefeli appreciated. "We still haven't tracked down that dratted poisoner."

"You have to take care." Jola pointed at Nefeli. "He wants to kill born compeers, not princesses."

"Yet he might sacrifice a princess to get a compeer." Nefeli caressed Jola's cheek. "I doubt there's anyone at court who doesn't know something of what you mean to me. Will you be my partner—as host and whatever else may come?"

Jola paused, swallowed hard, then gripped Nefeli tight. "Yes."

"Then that's what I'll tell my mother when I meet with her."

Relief flooded through Nefeli, followed an instant later by anxiety. Her toes twitched and fluid gurgled in her stomach. Flickers of pain along her skin offered reminder of her promise.

Jola didn't—couldn't—completely understand just how much their lives might change. Still, she'd agreed to the first alteration. Surely they'd have time to talk over any further while hosting the envoys and then on the trip back to Tharis

If Nefeli were to become Marchon someday, she wanted Jola at her side.

But only by her own choice.

❧ 8 ❧

Memory of the Shadow came back to haunt Jola after Nefeli left.

Jola strode around her lover's rooms. Her soft sandals trod a familiar tempo, stepping in the same spots over and over, though she hadn't worn through the rug. She added a half-step between full to vary the gentle thuds echoing for lack of other noises. Most sensible people took naps in the late afternoon heat and roused in time for dinner and evening delights.

She could be sleeping right now, except she'd left the bed sheets decidedly awry. A clean light blue tunic fluttered around her ankles, bound at her waist by a slender twined gold and silver cord. The silver thread in the trim of her matching mantle caught the light streaming through minute cracks in the closed shutters. A few tendrils of hair quivered against her cheeks, though she'd fastened the bulk on the top of her head.

The whole hardly made for a regal appearance despite the precious metal threads in her clothes. They suited her station as a princess, barely.

But soon she'd stand in the place of the Terparchon to welcome the Erevestisi.

Erevistisi.

The name alone made her breath catch in her throat. The mother who'd born her claimed a trader from one of their caravans as the likeliest to have sired her.

Such a distant, uncertain connection hardly made her one of them, but left her curious.

She'd host them, with Nefeli, but neither of them would likely need to do much. Courtiers and servants would arrange most of the details. Rooms for the guests. Meals.

Jola need only stand at Nefeli's side. Perhaps dance if the envoys wished to be honored with a small ball.

Though it wouldn't hurt to consult with the senior servants and librarians. Ensure the rooms matched known tastes and preferences of Erevestisi traders. Investigate accounts of their customs and food preferences. Her third mother, the leatherworker, had muttered about them preferring vegetables to meat, and sniffed whenever Jola turned up her nose at a choice cut.

Still, all that Jola could do with relative ease to make the envoys welcome.

Unfortunately, as a host she'd also have to accompany them to the site of the former Shadow of the Moon.

The thought alone seemed to make the walls narrow around her. The air turned warm and thick, better to drink than breathe. Tremors rippled through her limbs. She couldn't stay and walking in circles no longer eased her nerves.

Even this far gone in summer, it was hot enough that most of the palace and city rested or at least retreated indoors in the afternoon.

A good time for Jola to venture out on her own.

The door clicked shut. The hall lay empty save for a tall, broad-shouldered man leaning against the wall partway down. No helmet or blue-and-copper circlet adorned his dark brown curls. A simple dark red tunic fell from one shoulder to his ankles, above feet shod in plain sandals. The skirt folds nearly hid the long sheathed dagger hanging from his belt.. The style, popular with many of the servants, revealed an impressive musculature in exposed skin of copper brown.

Brenn's clothing differed so greatly from his usual uniform as a captain of the royal guard that Jola only recognized him after she'd nodded and turned away—and he'd fallen into step behind her. The solid slap of his sandals against the stone drowned out her footsteps, as he managed to match her pace.

"What are you doing?" she asked.

"Guarding you." Even when she slowed to start down the narrow back stairway, he remained one pace behind and slightly to the side.

She had to glance back to catch the merest hint of a smile twisting his lips. "You're on duty?"

"Of course."

"You think I need protection in the palace?" Stopping on the landing, she whirled around and set her hands on her hips.

"Natter was in the palace." Brenn angled to put the wall at his back. His head moved ceaselessly, checking up and down the stairs.

"He worked in the gardens, not the buildings. And he poisoned Idan, a compeer, not a princess." Jola continued down the stairs. The air was too close to linger long. "You should be guarding Nefeli."

"She had guards, in the palace and outside, and doesn't protest them," Brenn said. "We don't know all of what Natter did or who he sought to destroy other than Idan. He may not have worked alone. You're important, therefore the decision was made that you should be guarded."

"By whom?"

"The Terparchon." He darted around her to open the door and check the hall before allowing her through. "Do you want to challenge her over this?"

"No." A few steps down and she exited the royal residence, pausing to allow Brenn to check the empty courtyard for phantom—or real—threats. "But why you? Isn't this below your rank?"

"By some measures, yes, but . . . I am known to be friendly with some of the princesses and compeers." His sandals clacked against stone and gravel as he returned to her side. "Few will wonder at my being with you than a guard in uniform trailing on your heels."

She took small breaths, the better to adjust to the heat and humidity. Even in the shade of the arched entryway, the air had a heavy stillness that discouraged fast movement. Nearby a thin stream of water trickled out of a frog-faced fountain to pool in a narrow bowl before continuing on to the drain below. The dancing pavilion lay ahead to her right, on the rise above the lake, and the princesses residence stretched out to the left. Between them lay a wide passage with the bright greenery of gardens at the far end. "Are all the princesses being guarded?"

"All of the princesses are receiving some measure of protection."

"Explain." Dipping her fingers into the bowl, she swallowed a handful of warm but clean water.

"Some of the princesses are very well suited to defend themselves against most threats, and a guard unfamiliar with them would only get in their way."

"Such as?" She waved at the fountain. He paused long enough to check around before bending to drink.

"Melite, Iduma, Heron."

Jola nodded, unable to argue with any of the names. Adjusting her mantle so that a swathe of cloth covered her hair and offered a little protection between her and the bright sun, she set off down the passage.

"Where are we going?"

"The gardens."

He grunted, as though punched in the stomach. "Any one in particular?"

"You know."

Only a few others would guess straightaway: two princesses and the newest of the compeers, who also happened to be Brenn's brother. There were only five of them present the night that lightning struck the Shadow and left flowers behind.

She'd returned only once in the intervening weeks, that time in the company of Nefeli and several others. At least—Jola had walked there and stood and looked around but nearly the whole of the event formed a blur in her memory. Princesses and compeers were very good at reading body language, even if Nefeli had promised not to read anything Jola's feet leaked into the earth without permission, and Jola's head ached in remembrance of the effort required not to hint that she knew anything more than anyone else.

In a matter of days she'd repeat the not-showing-anything on her face not only with Nefeli but a group of strangers who wanted first and foremost to see the site.

Jola meant to see it herself, to truly absorb the sights and smells, beforehand. Rather fitting to do so with someone who also remembered the change.

His mouth tightened and a pulse beat at his temples, but he kept his opinions to himself.

The path through the woods seemed shorter than it had that not-so-long-ago night. A breeze danced through the woods, wicking away some of the sweat on her brow and arms.

The air carried a light, sweet aroma. The perfume of the flowers, which defied description save that the scent alone eased tension and loosened muscles she hadn't realized ached until they did so no longer.

One moment she trod stepping stones through bushes, the next she quivered at the edge of a wide clearing. Her gaze swept from the perimeter inward. A path traced the edge, each stone well-set and the surface clear of the blue-green mosses growing around.

More stone paths almost met near the center. No one else visited the flowers on this hot, sultry afternoon, but they had at better times of the day. Too many visitors had crossed the grass and moss filling the space between the stones. Their footsteps left behind bare spots, giving the once pristine clearing a dusting resemblance to ripped clothing awaiting mending.

Only the center truly flourished. There, glorious blooms of midnight blue and silver topped long stalks of matching blue, the leaves of deepest green. Every mote of the hard, bitter stone circle that resembled the full moon had melted away. Butterflies in myriad colors swooped and stooped around the petals.

Beautiful to see, but Jola closed her eyes anyway—the better to breathe deep. The perfume filled her, bringing a touch of the cool of night and easing ever-more tension from her muscles.

She hadn't liked the Shadow. Few people had admitted doing so in her hearing. Then again, common knowledge held that the Terparchon disdained the mass of dull white rock that had once rested within the center of the clearing. The current Terparchon, at least—her husband even more so—and Jola suspected some of the loud dismissals of the Shadow, past and present, had as much to do with gaining their favor.

Similar motives might have inspired favorable opinions under the previous Terparchon—blowing hot and cold to suit the weather and the ruling temperament. Jola hadn't joined the court until after the old ruler's death, and couldn't say for sure.

The flowers inspired admiration equal to dislike of the old Shadow. The similarly strong degree left Jola unwilling to trust the pleasure welling in her. Long before she'd become a princess, she'd spent hours tending gardens. Her family had mostly grown plants to eat, and occasionally trade, but they'd cultivated blooms for beauty around the edges.

Often the loveliest buds had the least perfume, and the simplest, most overlooked petals gave off the sweetest aroma.

Here appearance and scent matched.

And gave her heart, trusting or not, ease.

Lids heavy and low, she followed the stone paths. The urge to do as others had and dart across the open space tugged at her, but she resisted. Step by step she kept to the stones.

Brenn maintained pace behind her, stopping when she did. Only an arm's length separated her from the blooms. Stretch out, and she might brush the petals with her fingers. She pressed her arms tight against her sides.

"At least the Terparchon accepted the story that an odd bolt of lightning worked the change," Brenn said.

"It's the truth." Even if it had had help bolting down from the sky after a heavy storm.

"She did accept the answer, didn't she?"

"You just said that." She tore her gaze from the flowers to frown at him.

"It's what I've heard, but you might know better." He waved at the woods behind them, and the royal residence further back. "You have more to do with her."

"And yet I didn't know you'd be guarding me." Jola glared at him, then shook her head and sighed. "Nefeli hasn't said otherwise. According to Danissa and her big mouth," the other princess-witness had spoken out-of-turn, "the Terparchon knows a princess and a compeer were involved, but not who. No one else knows except those of us who were there, and that librarian Danissa's fallen for."

He grimaced as a bitter chuckle escaped him. "I had the funny idea we might be able to keep it all a secret."

"We kept enough, if the Terparchon is willing to forgo demanding names. For now."

Some of the flowers flared, their petals curving as their stalks bent and swayed. Jola's arms crossed over her chest as though she held a bouquet of them—or contained power as she had the other day. Only then did she realize she'd imagined the power in the form of flowers as she'd loosed it into the earth.

All of which sent prickles of unease along her spine. A surge of longing to be home, and far away from the summer palace, flowed through her. She forced it on, for she had no true choice but to remain with Nefeli and show the site to strangers.

No one really knew what had happened. Even Brenn's brother and Gisela, the princess he loved who'd Danced the change, admitted confusion. They'd only been trying to escape the poisonous white rock.

"Has your brother said anything more about that night?" After one last deep breath, Jola turned away and started back over the stepping stones. She refused to turn back, despite the wreaths of airy perfume wafting around her.

"Has Gisela?"

Jola's turn to grimace. "Only that she danced on instinct, and that she went there in the first place in a fit of anger over the old Terparchon's mistreatment of her people."

"He doesn't know how they did what they did either." The harder soles of Brenn's sandals clopped against the stones, ever-so-slightly off Jola's pace. "Isn't it the kind of thing you do in your underground chamber?"

"No." She stopped halfway to turn and take another glance. The flowers swayed in the breeze, as though summoning her. Her steps quickened in response. "I hope they, at least, escape here soon."

"They're going with the Marchon, as far as I'm aware."

"Good for them. And you?" She divided her attention between the conversation and the dwindling perfume of the flowers. Distance made it easier to view and smell without the desire to touch. More distance would be better, or some place with other distractions and scents. The infirmary, perhaps, and a visit to see how Solon faired.

"I'll be here, to guard you."

"And how long have you known that?"

"That I'll be staying? Several days. That you will be?" His mouth stretched in a wide grin. "That was a guess."

"Well you can guard me over to the infirmary." She wagged a teasing finger at Brenn. "Not to visit Ylena, mind you."

"Of course." He nodded, the epitome of a guard sworn to see nothing, hear nothing, say nothing, save keep his ward safe. Then the facade cracked. "How is she?"

"Doing better." She turned away, letting him regain his distance, and concentrated on choosing her steps.

Only to nearly run smack into Solon. The same man as the day before, except sweating heavily. The fringe of hair circling his crown stuck flat to his skin, drops sliding from the ends of each strand to streak his face and soak into his gray tunic. He wore no mantle though he shivered, and had likewise foregone sandals. His bare feet made only faint thuds against the earth.

Behind him and nearly in his shadow, despite being his equal in height, strode Amara. She too wore gray, tunic and mantle, a shade close to the silver of her long braid. Her lilac-colored skin better suited twilight and dawn than afternoon. Jola had heard whispered comments about her clothes giving her the look of one half-dead, but had always considered them equally appropriate for Amara. The bright golden light revealed how thin her skin had grown, as parchment stretched to the breaking point over a short nose and high cheekbones.

Even so, Amara managed to keep up with Solon without breaking into a sweat.

"Who let you out?" Jola stepped into Solon's way and waved at the damp spots marring his tunic.

"I'll recover faster in my own rooms. It's too noisy and crowded in the infirmary, people in and out all day and everyone who visits Ylena stops to see me too. Stefan, Todor, Zora, even Brenn." Solon came to a halt and turned up his nose, pointing at the guard. "Too many visitors. I'm not sick, I just need quiet."

"Truly?" Jola turned to face Amara.

Solon made a choked sound and swayed, but didn't make any move to pass.

"Wherever he can relax and rest is best." Amara patted Solon's shoulder, smiling at Jola although her eyes were dark and sad. "Burnout results in part from doing too much too fast on too little rest and resources. It leaves one vulnerable. Anything that undoes one of those knots will make things better."

"Give me my own room any day." Solon crossed his arms over his chest.

"Which this is not." Jola stepped aside, waving at the clearing.

"I wanted to see the flowers." He wrinkled his nose at Amara. "Alone."

"Go on," she said. "I'll wait here, so there'll be no one to catch you if you fall."

"I won't fall." He tottered a few steps forward.

The acrid scent of his sweat mingled with the flowers and turned the glorious scent into something harsh that hit the back of Jola's throat. She nearly choked, eyes watering. Amara clapped a hand over her mouth. Brenn coughed.

Only Solon seemed unaffected. He stopped, back to them, and squared his shoulders. Drew in a deep breath. "Gah, that's horrid. Tastes of ash."

Turning around, he pinched his nose and swallowed hard. "All right. I've seen it. I'm heading back to my rooms."

"Of course, lead the way." Amara stepped aside to let him pass, then fell into step with Jola behind. Brenn came last.

Solon set a slow pace. They walked in silence until well into the woods and away from the last vestiges of the floral perfume. Earthier scents replaced it—heavy, smoke sonnewood and mushrooms and animal scat—that softened the sharp edge of the sweat still pouring off Solon.

"I'm never Dancing above ground again," Solon's head drooped, voice soft enough Jola nearly missed the words.

"It's not the above ground part that's the problem." Amara tapped his shoulder. "It's cutting corners and pushing yourself."

"And age."

Amara nearly choked, jerking hard. "I provided more than thirty years of straight service, and I can still match you any day I choose."

Solon clomped on in silence for a moment before admitting, without turning, "and maybe I haven't been practicing as much as I should have." After which he shifted his head far enough to cast an eye on Jola. "Don't you do that."

"I'll try." Jola turned her hands out and pressed her lips together, the better to keep back sharper retorts that came to mind.

"More than try, since you're directing it now." He stopped and moved to the side of the trail, leaning against a sonnewood tree. His tunic fluttered and caught on the rough bark.

Amara took a few more steps.

"Whatever do you mean?" Jola drew up to her full height, arms close at her sides. Accidental or not, Solon, Amara, and Brenn formed a triangle around her.

"That's what you were doing, the other day." Solon held up a finger. "Told you I remembered. I'm not forgetting everything."

"What I did . . ." Jola's lungs seemed tight. Filling them required forcing air in and down.

"He said you drew the power from him and redirected it into the earth." Amara's arms fluttered together, mirroring the holding motion Jola had used, then opened again.

"Weren't you the one who told me not to tell anyone?" Jola glared at Solon.

"Amara isn't anyone."

Unable to argue with that, Jola tilted her head pointedly at Brenn. The guard stood loose and at ease a few paces behind. "And Brenn?"

"Oh, right." Wrinkles formed on Solon's brow, and he rubbed his temples. "I forgot him."

"He won't say anything to anyone, other than me, will you now?" Amara faced Brenn and laid a finger across her lips. He mirrored the action, one eyebrow quirking, and she smiled at Jola. "There, that's settled."

"I'm glad something is." Jola clasped her elbows. Lifting her chin, she nodded at Amara and tried to keep any hint of a plea from her voice. "So what did I do?"

The older woman shifted to mirror Jola's stance, down to the tightening of her lips as Jola recognized the dance technique. "What does the Terparchon do, when princesses dance and compeers guide?"

"She sends the power where it's needed." Jola drew in a hiccuping breath and let it out slowly. She opened her arms and a crackle of power rippled though she hadn't meant to summon anything. Sparkles flickered for a few moments, turning to ash as they fell. She'd seen the same around the Terparchon once or twice, though only when startled.

"That's what you did, albeit a more rudimentary way. Then again, it was your first time, was it not?" Amara scooped a handful of ashes and held them out.

Jola cupped her hands to receive the ashes. They still held minute sparks of light and carried a spicy flavor distantly familiar although Jola couldn't say from where. Time seemed to stretch and bend around her. One moment she stood at the center of the triangle, the next she was arm-in-arm with Amara following as Solon straggled back toward the princesses' residence.

"You'll get better if you practice." Amara squeezed Jola's arm.

"I'll get more practice?" Jola asked.

"Maybe. If all doesn't go awry as it has so often before. It, too, can lead to burnout." The Amara nodded at Solon, then laid a finger across her lips again. "But you must keep this quiet, just for now. Tell no one you don't trust in your bones until and unless the ability settles and stays."

"You're sharing it here." Though Jola already shared one deep secret with Brenn, what was another?

"Brenn is only half-listening, and he knows how to keep his mouth shut." Amara nodded back at the guard following them, then forward. "Solon knows more than he should, but is too busy keeping himself upright to make it to his chamber without help. That's all he'll remember of this walk. While I am more silent than the grave." She leaned in close. "Tell Nefeli, if you trust her. If you don't, then refuse the urge the next time it takes you. You may stand in the Terparchon's stead, and do well there, but remember that there can be only one Terparchon at a time."

Only one Terparchon. The words echoed in Jola's ears as she returned to Nefeli's rooms to dress for dinner. Her lover didn't show, or leave word. Still closeted with her mother, being officially offered the opportunity to represent the Marchon with her chosen princess at her side to represent the Terparchon.

A wondrous chance and a threat. Above all, Jola wanted Nefeli helping her puzzle through the way her dancing was changing.

༄ 9 ༄

Despite the last heat of summer, Nefeli's hands and feet chilled, thanks to heavy circlets adorning wrists and ankles. She wore neither her best nor her worst, nothing more or less than a sunny mantle over a purple tunic, and sandals touched with a matching yellow. Colors that her mother liked in general, and had complimented on Nefeli in specific. Cloth and leather fine, soft, and suited to the formal dinner of exquisite roasted vegetables and pastries whose aromas filled the halls and made Nefeli's stomach rumble.

She'd let Jola choose her clothes.

In her lover's honor, Nefeli had also dug out a set of bracelets and anklets—her mother's gift. The long ovals set with yellow beads dangling from her ears, however, came from Jola. The princess might accompany her in the flesh, but Nefeli preferred to keep remembrances of her close.

The narrow, shadowy hall seemed to leach heat from the metal. The afternoon warmth didn't reach here, or if it did it skipped over and around Nefeli.

Or, more likely, her blood cooled all around her in hope or dread.

Her mother kept her waiting. By choice or accident, since she wasn't alone. Two others stood with her in the room, whose steps

Nefeli couldn't mistake if she chose: her father, pacing, and her parents' trusted confidante and servant, the eleee Rik, standing close against the door.

Few of their words escaped, even as broken sounds.

Nefeli retreated all of three steps to the far wall and leaned back.

Waited.

And waited.

Her father left by an inner door, letting it slam behind him. Rik opened the outer, bowing and glancing sideways at Nefeli before slipping down the hallway. Tall and angular with a face made for smiling, they walked light on the earth despite their wiry hands carrying a basket filled with laundry.

With the door opened, Nefeli's nose twitched at a whiff of an airy, fruity perfume mingling with a light breeze bearing moisture from the lake. Her father disliked the odor, so her mother's use indicated irritation or anger at him although nothing came through her stance.

The room was bare in ways old and new. Old, for it had once been nothing save a passageway or waiting area between personal and public suites, with unmarked doors at either end. Unusually for the palace, the whitewashed walls and tiled floors were undecorated. The furniture had seen better days, chairs and tables bearing scuff marks although the seat cushions were regularly replaced to ensure comfortable seating. The far wall boasted the only adornment: long shutters folded back allowed an expansive view of the white-capped waves rolling across the lake.

As her mother's favored semi-private receiving area, it should be partly-filled with attendants. Not servants, but counselors. Amara or Idan, if the latter weren't still in the infirmary, or Rik or one of the half-dozen officials her mother relied upon.

Or at least one or both of Nefeli's siblings.

Instead, Nefeli had the ultimate honor: a personal interview with her mother.

Or with the Terparchon.

The older woman stood facing the closed door through which the Marchon had passed, presenting her long, narrow profile with deep-set eyes, thick black brows, and a thin-lipped mouth. Her burnished skin showed lines at her eyes and along her brow. A dark blue mantle nearly covered the paler blue of her tunic. The way she'd wrapped it meant the heavy gold-embroidered waves along the edges showed how her shoulders slumped. When she turned to Nefeli, no chimes marked her movement. The ruler who almost never went anywhere without a half-dozen or more bangles around wrists or ankles wore no jewelry, or sandals on her long feet either. She'd left bangles in a heap on a a table near her rooms, and her sandals abandoned below.

Only once before had Nefeli witnessed her mother in similar garb and pose. Memory of the older woman's expression that day, before she left to confront her own mother a last time, still sent chills down Nefeli's spine.

This time, at least, the face the Terparchon turned to her daughter showed fatigue rather than fury.

A moment later, signs of exhaustion vanished. Nefeli was welcomed. The Terparchon's torso jerked as though about to lurch forward for an embrace only to hold back. The older woman offered Nefeli a seat and choice of light refreshments despite the looming banquet later in the evening.

Both sat on chairs angled so as to offer a view of the lake and the other, neither eating or drinking.

Or speaking. Nefeli let her hands rest loose in her lap as her chest rose and fell in an even rhythm. Her mother's breathing almost matched hers, but her inhalations and exhalations were a hair shorter than Nefeli.

The Terparchon broke first. "What has your father told you?"

"What do you mean?" Nefeli lurched, grabbing the edges of her seat to brace herself. She could not resist checking her father's location —out pacing the palace walls.

"Surely he gave you warning, as he has before." A dark eyebrow lifted. "So?"

Nefeli licked her lips. "You're splitting the court. You and father will set off on your usual processions around the land, but part of the court will remain behind to host the Erevestisi envoys. You would like me and Jola to welcome them in the place of you and father."

"You and Jola." Her mother wove her fingers together and tilted her head back. "You've made your choice, then."

"Did you doubt it?" Nefeli straightened, feet flat on the floor and chin high.

"She had a tough time adjusting to being a princess, but ever since she's excelled." The Terparchon nodded. "You've made a fine choice."

"Thank you." A stray breeze circled the room, spreading the ruler's perfume far and wide. Nefeli's nose twitched and she pressed her lips together tight, resisting the urge to sneeze.

Again a long pause, with Nefeli determined to wait her mother out.

A thin smile twisted the older woman's lips. "And if she doesn't prove up to the task, she may step down and you choose another."

"There's confidence for you." Nefeli said.

"You are not married yet, only courting no matter how close you keep to each other, and even when you are bound you have options." The Terparchon dismissed Nefeli's words with an airy hand wave, then leaned forward. "Remember, your blood is the key. The inheritance passes through you. Whatever children you may share with her, only those to whom you give birth may one day take your and my place."

A lump formed in Nefeli's throat. She swallowed hard, but it stuck there. Energy whipped up and down her spine and her breath caught in her lungs until forced out. "You're not talking about the Erevestisi, are you?"

"That is only the beginning. I've waited as long as I could. I wanted you to have as much time and freedom as . . ." Her mother's shoulders slumped and exhaustion emanated from her for a moment, then she shook and sat straight again. "But the lack of formally named heirs is a weight the land can no longer easily bear."

"You waited for me?" Nefeli rubbed her chest. She'd hardly believed her father's warning that the offer would be made, and found far more difficult taking in the explanation of why it had been long in coming.

"Why not?"

"But Zora was your heir. Or Todor, once Ylena won him." Despite a suddenly dry mouth, swallow after swallow broke up the lump in her throat. Yet at the same time the tingling along her spine spread along her limbs.

"Has Ylena won him?" The Terparchon tilted her head to the side, lips pursed. "I've heard rumors their connection is breaking."

"If she knew she'd be the next Terparchon if they stay together, she'd surely make it happen." And what she'd do when she learned that wasn't the case—Nefeli could hope she'd be reasonable and accept failure to realize her ambition.

"Is that what you think I want for him, for any of you? Someone bent on staying because she wants what I have?" Her mother drew back, hurt flashing in her eyes.

"You smiled when she was courting him." Nefeli said.

"He deserves to be courted, but I wish him someone whom he wishes to court in equitable measure." A rueful expression wiped the hurt from the Terparchon's face. "Your father married me in no small part to gain the resources needed to ensure his people survived. I married him in large part to anger my mother. We both succeeded, but we set our sights too low. I desire more for Todor, Zora, and you—that you all court and be courted in balanced measure."

Nefeli's mouth snapped shut. Silence again, but not from her waiting her mother out. She had no words, struck by the intense vibrations rolling off her mother.

"So you may love whom you choose, marry whom you choose, do whatever you choose." The Terparchon added, leaning forward and peering at her daughter's face.

"Except serve as Terparchon." The wrong words, but the only ones to come to Nefeli's mind and slip out. A half-laugh escaped her, and she clapped a hand over her mouth.

"You can never be Terparchon. You've always known that and never cared." Her mother laughed too, a deep belly rippling sound.

True enough. Nefeli set her hands on the arms of her chair, the better to ground the tension in the wood. "I'm a born compeer. I know my worth."

"There has never, to my knowledge, been a Marchon who was born a compeer." The Terparchon said. "That will be something new."

No matter how many hours Nefeli had had to consider the possibility, it still rested uneasily on her shoulders. "If not Ylena and Todor, I thought you'd chose Zora to succeed you. Grandmother did."

"Your grandmother does not make my choices for me." The older woman stiffened.

"No, but Zora is a princess." Nefeli matched her mother's straight spine, then blinked and shook her head. "Mostly." The truth of her sister changed minute by minute, hour by hour. "There's one of her that isn't, and maybe a second. I've never been quite sure how many she is."

"After you proved to be a compeer, my mother was determined Zora would be a princess." The Terparchon threw up her hands. "The line has passed unbroken along the female line since the first Terparchon. Occasionally it went aunt to niece, but always only to the daughters of sisters. All were princesses. Mother refused to admit the possibility that none of her grandchildren might carry princess magic."

"She was right. At least three of Zora are princesses." Nefeli rubbed her forehead. She sent her power in search of her sister and found the younger woman down on the immense plaza facing the sea. Standing upon the mosaic of the first Terparchon. One of her controlled her body, but other selves clung close as shadows ever shifting and defying proper counting.

"None ever admits it. I will not pass the burden of ruling to someone who hides the very quality that would make them more desirable as an heir. I choose you." The Terparchon rose and held her hands above Nefeli's head. "Do you accept this?"

All thought and emotion drained from Nefeli, as if a great wave had washed over her. Emptiness ruled her for a moment, then certainty welled up. She could do this, with Jola at her side.

"Yes."

Her mother's hands rested heavy on her brow. Cool fingers brushed her forehead as the weight lifted.

The older woman resumed her seat, satisfaction blazing from her face. "That will keep to the bloodline, but allow for new and different dances. Just remember"—she wagged a finger—"it is your children who must inherit. Or Zora's, if she bears any. Jola's children may be given high honors, but not rulership in their own right."

"I understand." Nefeli nodded, letting the words enter her and storing them away for deeper consideration later.

"You may chose Jola to stand next to you in my stead, as you represent your father, when the Erevistisi visit—and then opt to marry someone else. That is your choice. I will welcome Jola, or whomever you decide upon."

Nefeli's arms pressed tight against her sides, but she plastered a pleasant smile on her face. *She* had no doubts. Her mother teased, surely. Nefeli arched an eyebrow, much thinner and lighter than her mother's but a clear mirroring of the older woman. "So long as they are a princess?"

"That would be simplest. But it is also possible you could find a princess willing to serve as Terparchon without being your partner." The other grimaced. "It's not a course I recommend, as you may find the court far more restive in such a case. More prone to resistance and plots than they normally are. There's a reason our ancestors usually ruled as married pairs. Still, when I am gone, I cannot hope to have any say."

"You really think I could marry one person and have another as my Terparchon?"

"No, but that doesn't mean you can't try. If I had had the option, I might have done so just to spite *my* mother." The Terparchon's lips pulled back to show sharp white teeth. "I never expected to be my mother's heir. I was the last and least of her children, until I became the only one to sprout princess magic."

An all-too familiar topic. Nefeli settled back, fingers rapping against the arms of her chair. Better to stop that line, even if it meant returning to a former matter. "What if Zora stops denying she's a princess?"

"I've made my choice." The Terparchon gestured at Nefeli, then wagged a finger again. "But you'd best be married to a princess in that event." Her gaze narrowed as she studiously checked the room before fixing it again on Nefeli. "You didn't bring Jola with you."

"I didn't know I could."

"You didn't ask. You didn't presume. As my heir, you will need to do both on occasion." Nefeli's mother rapped her fingers against her chair arms, smiling at her daughter to suggest the mirroring was intentional. "Under the circumstances, I will not formally announce you as your father's heir, nor name Jola as the next Terparchon yet. That shall wait until the court reunites at the winter palace. I will, however, make clear that you and your chosen princess stand in my and your father's stead in hosting the envoys and conclusions will be drawn from that. If you and Jola don't come to agreement soon, every unmatched princess —retired or not—may be after your hand."

The words ran through Nefeli's ears and rumbled in the back of her head, but was quickly set aside. She'd made her choice. But if she was indeed to rule, or even stand in her parents' stead for the Erevestisi alone—she needed to work with the Terparchon on how to divide the court into three parts. Who would go, who would stay—important questions required due consideration.

The warning didn't return to haunt Nefeli until much later, when the court gathered for the formal banquet. Long, narrow couches, covered with soft blue cushions stuffed with fresh grasses, formed half-circles facing a dais with a line of three couches boasting dark blue coverings. Tables between couches bore goblets filled by servants in pale gray tunics.

Nefeli knew where Jola was, on the couch they usually shared in the center, even before her gaze went there. Jola reclined on her side, with hem of her mantle properly spread out to show the silver fish embroidery. Further up, the sides of her mantle showed wrinkles where her fingers repeatedly gripped and loosened the falls of fabric. Yet a single bracelet circled her wrist, green jewels catching the light and making it easy to identify as one Nefeli had given her.

All of the royal councilors, princesses, and compeers were present and chattering away, their voices combining to override the distant murmur of the waves. Even Ylena had come from the infirmary. Lovely in a light purple tunic and matching mantle, the injured princess reclined on a light blue couch next to Heron, Zora's usual compeer. Ylena's crutches leaned against the wall behind her. Todor, a gloomy expression on his face, shared the far couch on the dais with Zora. The Marchon rested on the nearest, leaving the center for the Terparchon alone.

Before Nefeli could seek out the empty place next to Jola, her mother tapped her wrist and gestured minutely for her to follow All the way up to the dais. Not even to share her father's couch, but her mother's at the center.

"Rejoice with me," the chatter ended the instant the Terparchon's mellow tones rang out. "I bring you good news. As has been much rumored, the Governing Council of Erevestis has, indeed, requested leave to send envoys to visit here."

Heads nodded, smiles and frowns scattered throughout the crowd. The servants continued to circle, Rik pacing along the dais to ensure the Terparchon and Nefeli had full goblets, as well as her father and siblings. The sharp tang of the fruity liquid drove any and all mists from Nefeli's head. Her nerves twanged, but she stood tall despite being the cynosure of most eyes.

"Alas, our progress through the land cannot be put off." The Terparchon inclined her head graciously. "This once, we shall become three courts. Many of you will accompany me north, others go with the Marchon south and east, and some shall remain here with my beloved daughter, the compeer Nefeli and her chosen princess, whom I trust to stand in the Marchon's and my stead."

Zora's mouth opened in a wide O. Todor's brows pulled together in puzzlement. An odd light shone in Ylena's eyes,

Yet Jola turned away. Not in body, for her reclining posture changed little save for subtle indications of tensed muscles. Rather, her head tilted down and for the remainder of the feast her gaze avoided Nefeli.

❦   10   ❦

The announcement happened so fast. Jola had thought she'd have more time before. More chances to talk to Nefeli and explore what this would mean for them. What would change or not. Time to decide what to say, how to react.

Jola traced the silver fish embroidered on her mantle, glancing at the assembled masses from the corners of her eyes as servants passed out tray after tray of food. Berry-braised meat, marinated vegetable stalks, and bowls of creamy cold soup made the rounds. Red, green, and white, the colors stark against each other and the soft blue pottery.

Bits of words echoed in her ears, little understandable. Everyone was talking, or eating, and their voices blended into a massive noise that made her head ache. Even worse were the eyes watching her—some glancing, many smiling, others glaring.

She'd been a fool. Of course the Terparchon would share the news at the earliest opportunity, with so few days remaining before the court split and wound back to the winter palace. Those who were to remain with Nefeli needed to know, and keep out from under foot of the departures while making ready to host the envoys.

Yet before the Terparchon and Nefeli had arrived, whispers, hints, and rumors had rippled through the crowd that the Terparchon would announce not just who would stand in her stead for a few weeks, but her heir.

Jola should be excited for Nefeli. Her lover was finally receiving her due as the wonderful woman she was, the peerless compeer, dancer, leader.

But all Jola could feel was Nefeli slipping away—being pulled from Jola's side to take on duties that might part them. All the worse, when after the dinner the Terparchon did indeed summon Nefeli away to speak more in private.

Nefeli's hands gripped Jola tight. "Meet in my rooms, as soon as I can get away."

Jola shivered, tucking her hands under her arms, as Nefeli tripped away in her mother's wake. She slipped off through the crowd, face aching from smiling and nodding until she escaped into distant hallways.

Her rooms, Nefeli had said, not theirs.

Jola had never presumed they were hers as well. She'd waited for Nefeli to make it clear. Her lover was generous in sharing, welcoming Jola in all respects. Well, almost all respects, for she'd never actually asked Jola to share the rooms in the royal chamber and give up Jola's own place in the hall of the princesses. Nefeli encouraged Jola to be at home in her rooms, to keep clothing and trinkets there, but she hadn't said or made clear they were to share—at least, not in a clear way that Jola could accept and hold close and agree to. Or not that Jola had heard.

Even though Nefeli was so straightforward and decided. It was one of the things Jola admired most about her compeer and lover, the latter's ability to make a decision and stick to it. It was something innate to Nefeli, not even derived from her magic, for Jola knew several compeers less decisive.

Or maybe Jola hadn't listened close enough? She'd spent their first months, years, always sure that this wouldn't last, that she needed to be ready to leave . . . even as she'd luxuriated in it not ending, in their staying close, and hoped for more.

No, not just hoped. Nefeli *had* encouraged Jola earlier, asking her about being stand-in Terparchon to Nefeli's Marchon.

Jola to be Terparchon.

Jola, who's dancing had begun to change, grow . .. or turn dangerous, to be Terparchon for even a little time.

She nearly ran into a wall in shock. Bracing herself at the last moment, she set palms and forehead against warm stone. Even as she'd traced the embroidery on her mantle earlier, now she ran a finger along the smooth tiles set in the wall. Blues and greens blended into each other, forming a seascape all-too familier.

Jola hadn't paid sufficient attention to where she was going. She'd just shuffled through familiar corridors, and she'd headed the wrong way to *her* rooms, her dusty, musty, little-used rooms in the long hall with the other princesses's quarters.

Why hadn't Brenn commented on her going the wrong way?

A glance back, and the reason was clear. Jola had forgotten in the rush and worry of the banquet that her guard had changed. Brenn had left her with an equally tall, broad figure clad in tunic and skirt with a hint of copper rank at their ankles. Someone whom she'd seen around but rarely spoken to. She couldn't even remember their name and their glum, silent demeanor hardly encouraged conversation. They didn't even react to her stopping against the wall, or her glancing at them— merely raised an eyebrow and waited.

Perfumed air, bitter on the tongue, wafted from a nearby room through the open transom over the door that allowed air to circulate. Soft voices murmured on the other side, with the clink of mugs. A round of laughter burst from a chamber at the far end of the hall, then settled back into general quiet.

A door creaked open a few steps down. Amara slipped out of a suite of rooms—Solon's, of course, as the princesses generally took the same chambers year after year.

Amara had been at the banquet, surely? Her bright blue tunic and silver mantle, both colors perfect complements to her pale lavender skin, were suited to the festive occasion. Yet here she stood, where she no longer had chambers, holding a tall flask half-full by the way the green glass glinted in the light.

"How is he?" Jola wrinkled her nose as the hint of soothing balm wafting from the flask mingled with the too-strong perfume.

"Better for the rest, and I've given him something to help him sleep a while longer." Amara tapped the flask, head bobbing as she studied Jola. "You look to be in need of some yourself."

She held out the flask.

The scent grew stronger, overpowering the distant perfume and far more welcome.

Every ache and pain in Jola's body suddenly impinged upon her: temples throbbing, ache in back of head, even the dull pulse in her legs and heels from earlier dance practice. She longed for bed and time to lay aside cares.

But she still had to talk to Nefeli, and she wanted to do so in full possession of her senses.

Amara nodded, but slipped flask into Jola's hand all the same. "For when you need it."

Jola stared at the flask. Not if, when.

Amara turned and headed down the hall, only to pause and lay a hand on Jola's arm. Her gaze flicked over Jola's shoulder at guard, then Amara gave a meaningful glance at Solon's door. "Be careful, but also be sure to enjoy. Congratulations, and please give the same to Nefeli when you see her."

So much contained in so few words, but so much missing too. Be careful of what?

Jola held the flask against her side as she shuffled down the hall and through the twists that lead to the royal residence. For all that Jola had walked unthinking to her own rooms, she could do the same to Nefeli's rooms even were she blindfolded.

Then paused outside, studying the shadows and lines carved into the wood. Every door was different and unique. Several bore trees, but none with the breadth and careful attention to detail of the immense, impossible tree featuring leaves that in truth grew on a dozen different trees.

With a few heavy thuds, Jola's guard shifted to stand on one side of the door balancing the guard on the other.

The guard on the other.

Jola opened the door, latch clicking but the well-balanced weight swinging easily as it wasn't locked. Drawing in a deep breath, she entered and let it swing shut behind. She leaned back against the warm, solid mass.

Ahead, Nefeli paced in a small-tight circle. The skirts of her tunic and mantle flowed around her ankles, snapping as she turned back and forth.

One, two, three, and then she stopped. Visibly swallowed. Turned to face Jola with her features blank save for a hint of moisture in her eyes.

Regret pierced Jola. All her thoughts had been for herself, and she'd neglected the most important things. Stepping away from the door, she opened her arms and tried to let all her pride and delight in Nefeli's ascent show. "Congratulations."

"Truly?" Nefeli's shoulders were stiff, arms tight against her side.

"You know I mean it." She walked forward in full awareness Nefeli could read her steps, concentrating on her pride and pleasure.

Nefeli stayed in place, making Jola come to her—or perhaps she was unsure for once? Worse, her tension was likely due in no small part to Jola's fears, spilling over and causing grief.

This was Jola's lover, but also likely her future ruler. Jola knew how to greet the one, but not the other. Shivering, she set the flask on a table and went over to wrap her arms around Nefeli and hold her close. Their bodies warm and soft, readily aligning so that either head could easily lean against a shoulder. Hints of tension remained, slowly draining from Nefeli.

Jola's lover pulled back and cupped Jola's face in warm hands.

The hold was light and lacking in pressure. Jola didn't have to meet Nefeli's gaze eye-to-eye, but Nefeli would know if Jola tried to avoid it. She didn't.

Nefeli's warm brown eyes held puzzlement and uncertainty, unusual for her. "You wouldn't look at me earlier."

"It's not what you think," Jola sighed, "it's not because you're . . ."

"Tell me," Nefeli winced the instant the insisted words escaped her, and shook her head, then added in softer tones, "share with me, please."

"So many things."

"We have time." Nefeli said. "If I have to hold that door closed and the world on the other side I will, if you'll just trust me."

"I do." Jola laid her hands over Nefeli's, twining their fingers.

"You agreed earlier to stand with me in my parents' place, to host the Erevestisi." Nefeli asked. "Are you still willing?

"Yes." Jola put all her willingness into the words, her eagerness to be what Nefeli needed.

"Then what is wrong?"

The whispers from earlier, about Nefeli being more than a temporary stand-in for her parents rushed back over Jola. Mingled with them were memories of Amara cautioning Jola to be careful.

"What?" Nefeli asked.

"Is hosting the Erevestisi all that your mother asked of you?" Jola bit her lip, studying her lover close.

Nefeli pulled back slightly and studied Jola.

Jola shifted weight from foot to foot, not sure what Nefeli might be reading. Her lover tried not to take undue advantage through her gift, but had also admitted it was hard not tracking, knowing who was around and their general mood.

"She offered more," Nefeli said, "to name me as father's heir, and my chosen princess as hers."

Tension wracked Jola, and her body cooled—but Nefeli grabbed her hands, holding them with warm fingers.

"That's you, of course, but only if you're willing."

A headachy mixture of hope and delight rippled through Jola. That Nefeli continued to want her by her side, but could Jola be what her lover needed? Amara had warned Jola about her power possibly growing, or destroying her as Solon's was. No telling which.

"You will be a wonderful Marchon, better than your father." Jola hugged Nefeli.

"That's . . . you're partial." A blush stained Nefeli's cheeks as she smiled, though a hint of worry lingered in her eyes.

"It's truth." Jola said.

"And you?" Nefeli asked.

Jola couldn't pretend she didn't understand. "I don't know if I can be Terparchon, if I can Dance that long and not burn out."

"You don't have to decide yet," Nefeli squeezed Jola's hands. "Stand next to me after she leaves, and see how things go."

"It's not just that, it's leading the Dance."

"You can learn that. Mother did." Nefeli said.

Jola tried to find words to explain, but this was all wrong. She should be showering Nefeli with praise and comfort, not the other way around.

Amara had advised Jola to wait until her Dancing settled, but how would Jola know?

Still, she could wait a little longer, through a practice or two, and see if it even happened again. There was only that once, and that only because Solon's actions made it necessary!

So she'd agree to stand by Nefeli's side now, and hope for the best for later.

No, not just hope, make it happen.

Nefeli watched the moonlight slowly shift across the bed. The night breeze danced through the window, holding a touch of chill. She tucked the covers over Jola's shoulders and her own, wincing at the signs of stress clear on Jola's face even in the shadows.

Their conversation echoed in Nefeli's ears over and over, her own words in particular. She'd promised Jola the choice of whether or not to stand next to Nefeli as the land's next rulers. Yet had Nefeli pushed her too much?

Nefeli wasn't like Ylena, imposing her wants on her lover.

Yet the idea had sunk in, insidious, and flowed in her veins as sure as poison.

None of this was like Nefeli. She wasn't one to turn thoughts over and over, to rethink things, worry about what she'd said and done that could never be unsaid or undone. She moved forward, glancing back only to keep her way, made decisions, took, action, accepted consequences.

And didn't lie awake in the night worrying.

Nefeli's mother had offered her the heirship in such terms as made it clear that Nefeli was the rational choice. Nefeli agreed. It wasn't something she'd sought, though already ideas had begun to bubble within her of ways to support and encourage the tangle of connections between the land's separate parts. Still, Nefeli would have been amenable to being overlooked, despite being the eldest, if one of her siblings was better suited. But Todor lacked the strength and Zora was unpredictable . . .

And standing outside Nefeli's door.

Nefeli sat up in bed, careful to not disturb Jola. Her senses extended throughout the surrounding rooms and the long hall, checking for who was where though she could best locate those standing in the night: the guards to either side her door, and others further down guarding her parents and siblings' quarters. No sense of trouble from any.

Nevertheless, Zora was right outside, in the middle of the hallway with her body positioned as though ready to head on down but her head turned to one side.

Which Zora? Not one, or two, but at least three of the different individuals who comprised Nefeli's sister, maybe even the fourth, all arguing? Pushing at each other, or something, for the sense of their presences flickered from one to another too fast for Nefeli to know in truth who was there.

Until one pushed the others away. The main sister, the only one who wasn't a princess, turned and staggered away.

Nefeli slipped from under the covers and tucked herself into the far corner, where she had a stark, angled view of the chambers at the far end of the hall, where they jutted out in a tower. Golden light glinted. A soft mumble pulled Nefeli's attention away, as Jola turned and flung a hand over where Nefeli had lain. Nefeli's lover's lips turned down in a frown, visible in the soft moonlight, but she didn't wake.

Nefeli shivered. Unease? The chill of the night, especially as her feet were bare against the cool stone?

The gold light from her sister's rooms flickered and ceased, but Nefeli stayed at the window gazing out at the land she would someday rule.

She'd held her power so close for so long, ever since she was little. Who was it who'd told her, convinced her, it was best not to track people or at least not let them know you were tracking them? Better to save it for the Dance, or in matters of life and death.

Maybe it was her mother's friend and counselor, and Nefeli's fellow born-compeer Idan who'd admonished her to keep her mind to herself and her mouth shut. Or Amara, because that old princess knew nearly everything there was to know about Dancing. Or Rik, or her father, or one of the half-dozen or so born compeers who'd come, Danced, and burned out too fast.

But if Nefeli was to rule, she could let her magic flow free. Perhaps not all the time, no, she understood that people needed to keep some things to themselves, and it would take too much of her. Yet more than merely keeping aware of who was around her, keeping guard over herself and Jola.

Swallowing hard, she slipped the tight hold and her powers swirled in circles out from her. No longer was she limited to knowing only those who stood, but everyone around from side to side and on higher and lower floors.

Who was where, with whom or alone. So many lives and so many bodies pressing against the earth one way or another. So many hearts beating.

Nefeli didn't make any demands on her magic, just let it be.

Unsurprisingly, the first awareness of details focused on her family.

Jola sleeping, mouth agape, and hand rubbing the sheet where Nefeli had lain.

Nefeli's mother pacing in her room.

Her father lying on the cot in the small room where he'd met Nefeli, but no more asleep than her mother.

Zora curled into a ball in her bed, shivering.

Todor alone save for his guards in the shadows, out in the woods watching the glowing flowers that had once been a Shadow of the Moon.

Of all those Nefeli loved the most, only Jola slept—except she woke, too.

Nefeli remained in the corner, by the window, hardly looking at the moonscape as her power ensured she felt the hundreds, thousands of hearts beating in the city and across the land, and even across the lake on the far shore where others ruled.

Despite awareness of hearts in the distance, she didn't miss the rustle and soft footsteps as Hola left her bed, or the flow of air around the lean body as her lover slipped around the room before joining her at the window.

Jola laid a warm mantle across Nefeli's shoulders and dropped slippers to the side.

Nefeli shivered not from cold, but from the care, as she donned the slippers and held the mantle wide so Jola could slip under it as well.

"I should have told you earlier that your mother made the right choice." Jola wrapped her arms around Nefeli's waist. "You'll be wonderful, standing in her stead, and as her heir. I can't think of anyone else so well-suited."

"Not even my siblings or Ylena?"

Jola squeezed her tight. "You know your own worth so well, I don't always think to say how much I admire in you. But I do. Your decisiveness, your integrity, your care for everyone who crosses your path."

Muscles in Nefeli's back that she hadn't realized were still tense relaxed, her whole body flushing with pleasure. "You trust me that much?"

"Always."

"Can you trust my belief in you?" Nefeli turned her back on the window and the hearts outside to focus on the one closest.

"Yes." Jola nodded, but shadows lingered in her face and not merely due to the shifting away of moonlight.

"But?"

I trust, but I fear . . ." Jola cupped Nefeli's face, just as Nefeli had earlier. "But I don't want this to be about my fears, not now. Not tonight, when you're still in the first flush of realizing what you may be." Jola nodded at the window and the world awaiting. "Let everything else wait until tomorrow – for now, let me show you how proud and pleased I am for you."

For this moment, only Jola mattered—that she took the lead, started the kiss, and drew Nefeli back to their bed to tangle together.

❧　12　❧

Jola held her head high and shoulders straight as she glanced at her reflection in the oval mirror. The polished bronze dulled her orange mantle and soft green tunic underneath. Sandals with orange ribbons were visible under the fall of her skirts. Others might wince at the bright colors she preferred, but she would wear what she liked no matter how she looked. No matter how high she rose, she would not change that. Nevertheless, she did take moments to squint and make sure her hair was neatly pulled back and tied with a ribbon at her nape, that no stains or rents marred her clothes, and that her mantle was well aligned over her tunic.

She'd even donned the jangling gold bracelets and matching chain necklace Nefeli had given her the year previous—and the gold and silver cords across her brow marking her as a princess.

Surely Nefeli would approve, though she was not present to see. She'd gone off to consult with her parents on any of a thousand matters to be settled before the rulers set off on their rounds.

The bedclothes remained in a tangle, mute witness to the night's pleasure. Despite the warming morning air wafting in through the open window, redolent of late summer flowers, the soft mattress held no allure for Jola. Thuds and grunts flowed in along with the breeze, attesting to servants preparing the carts that would carry most of the court away.

The room felt empty without Nefeli, yet for the first time in a while it seemed to belong a little more to her and a little less just to Nefeli.

Maybe.

Nefeli wanted Jola at her side, that was clear. Though the compeer didn't know, yet, of the risk Jola would burn out. Yet Jola had only had an episode once. No certainty it would happen again, especially if she could stay well away from Solon.

But there were other matters to be settled, if Jola was to partner Nefeli in all ways—and some were best done one on one, without royal eyes watching, ears listening, or mouths interrupting.

Jola twitched, fingers plucking at her mantle.

Throwing her head back, she swallowed. Turned. Marched to the door and thrust it open.

Brenn stood to one side He turned and bowed from the waist, head tilted to the side.

Rubbing her temples, Jola studied him. His uniform sat perfectly fitted to his body with few creases and barely a speck of dust. His cords of rank gleamed at his ankles.

He was guarding her again, despite having risen in the palace guards high enough he could send others. "Isn't there anyone else you trust with my safety?"

"Of course." Brenn said as he fell in step with her. "I wasn't here all night, and I will not accompany you all the day, but matters are unsettled enough with all the changes to be made that I see this as a proper allocation of my time." A few steps later, he added under his breath, "with the added good that it keeps me away from the havoc of the preparations to depart, and the endless dragging of trunks one way and another."

"Ah." A glance down the hall leading to the princesses' rooms offered examples of what he fled from. Voices calling, the scrape of wood and metal against stone . . . one joy of staying behind was that Jola didn't have to sort her belongings and pack just yet. "But are you sure you want to guard me now?"

"This is my current duty." He stood straighter, if that was possible, and didn't ask but the silence hung heavy for a few breaths.

"I'm going to the infirmary." Jola ducked through an arch and started down the stairs. One hand rested on the smooth railing, the heels of her sandals slapping against the stone with each step.

Brenn's pause stretched five heavy thuds of his feet long, until he broke it. "Before breaking your fast?"

Jola's stomach rumbled, more felt than heard under the clatter of their steps. Likewise, she knew the roiling in her belly was as much or more dread as hunger. "First thing."

"Makes sense." Brenn nodded. "Get things clear with her, and you have a chance of winning her to your side."

"You think?" Jola wasn't sure whether to be pleased or concerned that he'd so easily guessed whom she went to meet. There was a compeer and several courtiers also currently staying at the infirmary, any of whom she could go see—and all of whom she'd rather under the circumstances.

"It's long odds, but worth a shot." He waved in the direction of the infirmary as they exited the stairs "As you will."

"Are you certain you don't want someone else to accompany me?" She stopped and set her hands on her hips.

"My task is to guard you, yours is not to guard me."

Jola bowed her head, lips tight at the unspoken rebuke. With a jerk, she headed off aware that she had trespassed somehow. In a low voice, glancing at him to be sure he knew the words were for him, she said "I'm sorry."

A half-smile flitted over Brenn's face as he repeated his words but in gentler tones. His job was to protect her, and he didn't want her worrying about him.

Though she'd rather worry about that than what lay ahead.

The usual route to the infirmary was fairly straight, a matter of passing through a number of halls and plazas. This time, everywhere there were signs of great commotion. Courtiers dashed here and there, scribes ticked off items consigned to storage, and the permanent servants struggled within the havoc to maintain some order against the upcoming visitation.

A good third of the infirmary staff were among those who never traveled with the court and always stayed behind. This made the infirmary one of the calmest places in the complex, and almost a joy to walk through as Jola consulted briefly with the infirmary administrators about equitable divisions of supplies and what might be expected of the Erevestisi envoys, in case one needed care.

Yet all Jola's calm and ease drained away the instant she left the administrators and passed through the doorway into the small garden at the center. Greenery abounded, ivies with touches of yellow and purple and oranges as sweet flowers and savory herbs perfumed the air from raised beds and baskets fastened to the walls. Water trickled, unseen for the central focus of the courtyard was the trunk of an old tree, polished to a fare-thee-well.

A chair had been placed directly in front of the trunk, on the gray flagstones. Ylena waited there, dressed in pale gray and with her bound leg raised on a pile of pillows precariously perched on a stool.

All Jola's brief calm seeped away and tension vibrated in her bones and teeth.

Ylena's chair was perfectly situated, facing the entrance and with no other chair anywhere in sight, only a few benches scattered around. If Jola wanted to sit and speak with her, she'd have to request a chair be brought with the attendant fuss and delay.

Here and now, Ylena reigned, even if she couldn't move far on her own.

Brenn remained just outside the entrance. He whispered "good luck" as Jola strode forward.

"Welcome." Ylena nodded at the nearest bench, set at an awkward angle to the chair. "Have a seat. Always so nice to have a visitor."

Jola nodded, but remained standing. "Have you been lonely?"

"How could I be lonely, when I am so well taken care of by the healers, and with princesses and compeers stopping by so regularly, as if on a schedule."

"We care." Jola pressed a hand to her heart. Both knew who'd set the schedule and ensured no one skipped their appointed visits.

"Here but for the grace of the wind would be you." Ylena waved at her leg.

"True enough. Sooner or later every princess suffers some injury." A shiver rippled through Jola. Had the earth sighed beneath, or was she imagining the movement? She widened her stance, planting her feet in hopes to remain steady.

"One falls, another rises."

"It still could be you." Jola clapped her hands. Enough of dancing around the true matter at hand, Ylena's likely futile hopes to rule with Todor. "Nefeli has asked me to stand at her side while she hosts the Erevestisi, but there are no guarantees beyond that."

Ylena's shoulders rounded and she shook her head. "I can tell a tree from a forest. The Terparchon will never chose her son to follow after her, no matter how strong a pair we made, and we didn't. I'll cut my losses and seek another way." She lifted her chin, gaze level. "Congratulations. I hope you'll both be very happy."

"Try saying that as if you actually mean it." Despite the distance, Brenn's soft voice came through clearly.

Ylena's cheeks turned bright red. She glared at him for a moment, then lifted her chin and fixed her gaze on Jola.

Jola twisted her fingers in her mantle and tunic skirt and settled onto the bench after all, back straight and body angled to face her fellow princess as though this were a dance. A thrum of power rippled through the ground. Ylena's good leg twitched, as she clearly felt it too.

"Why do you want to rule?" Jola asked.

"Why do you think?" The color in Ylena's cheeks remained high.

Jola studied the other. "Not power."

"What?"

"I thought that for a long time, but no longer." Jola tapped a finger, then moved on to the next. "Ambition, yes, to be the best, but it's not that that burns you now, is it?"

"Why do you want to know?" The other princess's shoulders pulled inward, tension clear in the lines of her arms and back.

"To do my best by you." Jola said. "I cannot offer you my place. That would not be honest or kind to you or Nefeli."

"I wouldn't want it. I'm one of those oddlings who prefers only men." Ylena's gaze flickered in Brenn's direction, but so brief Jola almost missed it.

Jola shrugged. She preferred to say she loved the person inside first and only after delighted in the outer wrapping, but to each their own. "But I can offer you *a* place, if I know what it is you want." And Jola wanted Ylena working with her and Nefeli, supporting Nefeli, and giving Nefeli the best chance to succeed rather than resenting and working against her.

"What do *you* want?" Ylena drummed her fingers against her sound leg.

"To belong." The words sprang to Jola's tongue, but under Ylena's gaze they didn't seem to be the whole truth. They weren't enough. She needed to offer more to ensure equal honesty in return. "To be a part of something bigger than myself. To do what I can to make things better." Energy rippled through her, the same satisfaction as at the end of a successful Dance. She sat taller, lighter, confidence bubbling up that she was stretching and reaching and becoming more, becoming someone able to stand beside Nefeli and bear a share of the weight of rulership.

Lowering her head, Jola leveled a stern glance at Ylena. She would have the same frankness in reply or nothing. "You?"

"To be able to make decisions for myself, rather than have them made for me." Ylena flashed back, then looked away. In a smaller voice, quavering on the last word, she added, "to be safe."

"I don't know what I can promise, but I'll do what I can." Jola rose and walked to stand at the other princess's side, offering her hand. "If the Terparchon chooses you to remain here when she leaves" and they both knew that was likely, giving Ylena more time to heal before making the long trek north, "and if there should be a dance, will you dance with us?"

After a moment's pause, Ylena matched Jola's hand palm to palm.

"I won't stand beside you when the Erevestisi arrive." Ylena waved at leg, grimacing at her own joke, "but otherwise . . . I'll dance with you for them, if that's needed, and I'll even go with you when you take them to see the former Shadow." Her chest jerked in a dry laugh. "Might as well see it myself."

Jola smiled, but her insides seemed to turn into a knot.

The former Shadow. She'd almost forgotten that was why the Erevestisi were sending envoys to see what it had become.

Jola still hadn't told Nefeli that she'd been there when it changed. In the distance, Brenn's face seemed cast in stone, no doubt also thinking of the night they'd both stood witness to strange power beyond comprehension.

Something they'd promised to keep secret, and had. No matter that the general lines had gotten out, only the five of them knew exactly who'd been there and done what.

But if Jola didn't tell Nefeli, that risked leaving her lover at a disadvantage when the Erevestisi arrived. She left the infirmary determined to do so—or at least to share what she could and hint at the rest. Whatever she could manage without breaking her word.

Except the moment she stepped outside the door, she plunged into the full chaos of departure preparations—with Nefeli in constant demand to answer questions or make decisions, and Jola only slightly less so.

And time slipped away.

❧ 13 ❧

Nefeli rested her hands on the stone railing edging the palace ramparts. High above the crowds filling the courtyard and spilling into the streets outside, she had cool, fresh air to breathe and space to either side. Despite the weights sewn into the hem of her deep blue mantle that should hold down tunic as well, her skirts fluttered in the breeze. The sun beat down, raising a layer of perspiration from her sandaled feet to her head under a woven straw hat whose wide brim rippled and flapped.

To either side, gaily clad princesses, compeers, courtiers, and servants formed a loose line. Jola to one side of Nefeli, Todor at the far end, and even the aged, retired compeer Idan had come down from his family's home in the hills to bid the court farewell.

All stood witness to the departure of the Marchon and his entourage. As always, Nefeli was amazed at how swiftly outright chaos resolved into an almost-organized clump of walkers leading the way, followed by heavily-laden wagons and laggards trailing behind. Guards ranged before, alongside, and aft.

So different seen from above rather than in the middle or at the forefront! The vantage point offered a clearer picture of the dust kicked up by feet, hooves, and wheels. No wonder those at the back of the train regularly complained. Likewise, it was easier to see who delayed and waited to the last, one person pushing it so long that they wound up racing through clouds of dust to catch up with the rearguard and the last wagons.

The distance lessened—but didn't hide—the constant, ear-aching clamor, from the grunts of the oxen as they pull the heavily laden wagons, wheels creaking of which at least one was bound to crack or break before the end of the day, and the thud of so many feet tromping against hard-packed earth.

Gold glinted at her father's wrists as he turned to wave one last time, or so it seemed. Nefeli couldn't be sure across the distance, though if she stretched her senses through the ground beneath she could match up his feet with that spot. The energy drain wasn't worth the reward, with too many people all in motion.

Her mother had gone two days earlier, taking the northern route with her third of the court. Her father was almost out of sight, with Zora & Amara at his side.

Much as she'd miss them, Nefeli admitted to a slight feeling of relief. It would be, should be, easier with them gone, not least because everyone had kept taking time out of packing to give her last minute advice upon advice, often contradictory, and sometimes practically unintelligible.

Jola sighed. The wind whisked the sound away, but Nefeli couldn't miss the rise and fall of her lover's shoulders.

"Wishing you were with them?" Nefeli asked.

"No, not for worlds." Jola's eyes sparkled as she moved closer to Nefeli, where the wind couldn't rob Nefeli of the princess's words. "I counted it out, and unless the Erevestisi stay here forever, there's every chance that taking the straight route we'll beat everyone else back to the winter palace. I'll see my family sooner than not! And, of course—" her lips softened in a sweet smile. "I'm here with you."

Nefeli smiled back and started to speak, only to stop and frown as Jola drew a deep breath and straightened. The princess's stance shifted, feet trembling against the stones beneath them.

They'd had so little time together since the decision to remain. All the waking hours each were pulled in a dozen different directions making decisions about supplies, housing, and all the details that had never needed to be settled before because the court always left in two entourages to circle the land but never before was a third left behind.

Nefeli had thought Jola's tension mostly due to her part in making those decisions—the need to undertake new responsibilities—but now that the rest of court was gone, her lover twitched and bit her lip, then threw her head back and met Nefeli's gaze square.

Yet her stance conveyed a degree of fear.

"I've been meaning to tell you. Promised myself I'd take the first opportunity, before the Erevestisi arrive . . ." Jola licked her lips. "About the Shadow, the former Shadow . . ."

"Yes?"

"You should know . . ." Jola's voice dropped lower, sounds barely reaching Nefeli. "I was there."

"When?" Nefeli blinked, unclear.

"Then."

It took Nefeli longer than she liked to realize what *then* mattered enough to justify a nervous confession: the change from Shadow to former Shadow. Which Nefeli had heard was the result of a lightning strike. A natural, if uncanny, accident. Or not. "How?"

"As a witness." Jola held still, face turned to the side and body tense.

"You never said you were there. Not even to me." Nor dropped any word as to why she'd have been there. Nefeli's throat was dry and she wished herself anywhere but high on the palace walls in full view of the remaining court.

"There were others there. We promised to keep silence, though one told the librarian who came to investigate, but kept the rest of our names secret." She gulped, glancing away at the courtiers and servants still waving at their departing friends and family members, then back. "We were afraid the Terparchon would be angry at all of us, for not preserving the Shadow."

"My mother wouldn't . . ." Nefeli grimaced and swallowed, frowning. She hadn't guessed how her mother would react, hadn't expected the Terparchon to be so full of fear that the destruction of the Shadow portended an attack on Codaros. Yet only after the librarian who investigated had convinced her the destruction didn't pose a danger had she decided to let the matter go. "It went well enough. You could have said something sooner." Something to *her*.

"I didn't want to made you complicit." Jola said, meeting Nefeli's gaze straight on and standing more confidently.

"I wish you hadn't . . . but I can accept that you chose that then." Nefeli crossed her arms over her chest, never looking away from her lover. "In the future, let me decide for myself."

Jola sighed, tension draining from her shoulders. "We weren't certain how people would react, especially after all the wars your grandmother fought to control them."

The mere thought of Nefeli's grandmother made her wince. The old Terparchon probably would have had anyone involved—even as witnesses—killed outright or tortured first. Nefeli didn't miss the woman at all, especially given the way so many servants and courtiers continued to act as though she were around and watching over their shoulders in disapproval, Nefeli included sometimes, to her regret. The reference did, at least, leave Nefeli less resentful over Jola's keeping secrets. A little, maybe. She grabbed Jola's hand and squeezed it.

Jola drew near, and Nefeli wished again they weren't on the palace walls—the more so when Jola's gaze shifted and there was a sudden disturbance of air and footsteps approaching behind Nefeli.

Todor turned his back on the last of the Marchon's escort and leaned against the wall, showing no awareness that he'd interrupted anything of import. His tunic and mantle barely rippled around him, a few drops falling from sopped hems.

"Well, they're gone. Good riddance."

Nefeli studied him, sensing more surprise from Jola's stance than from her brother. He exuded only dull exhaustion. "Whatever brought that on?"

"The prospect of several weeks without mother or father or Zora sticking their noses into my business." Todor wiped his forehead. The bright sun clearly revealed deep bags under his eyes.

Nefeli hadn't seen much of him in the chaos of packing and all her meetings with mother. His lank posture offered a study in fatigue and yet beneath lay a welter of conflicting emotions too tangled to be easily read unless she used more magic than usual, for which she preferred to have permission but all her family had refused it back when they first realized she was a born compeer and never changed their minds.

"What's wrong." A glance around showed some courtiers seeking permission to leave the wall. Nefeli waved for them to depart.

Todor waited. Only Nefeli, Jola, and their guards and the usual sentries keeping watch remained nearby, although farther down were Solon and his usual compeer, Leta, a large woman a little older than Nefeli and Jola. "You might as well be first to know, unless Ylena's been telling others before she told me. We're no longer a pair."

Nefeli stiffened, Jola's shock clear at her side. The news wasn't unexpected, but sooner than Nefeli would have predicted. Concern for her brother warred with the need to consider the impact on the remaining section of court. She wavered until Jola's touch on Nefeli's shoulder urged her forward.

"I'm sorry to hear that." Nefeli moved to hold him, but he stood board-stiff and so she held back. "If you ever wish to talk, or sit in silence, let me know."

"Maybe." Todor shrugged.

"I'm sorry too." Jola frowned and asked, "will you dance with her, or would you prefer a different partner?"

"Are there enough of us for a choice?" Todor's eyes were dark and tear-slick as he turned to her.

"Three princesses other than me: Danissa, Solon, and Ylena." Jola raised four fingers on each hand. "Three compeers other than your sister: you, Idan, and Leta."

"And Ylena and Idan both on the injured list." Todor said.

"But able, if needed. We'll pair them together, and you can partner Danissa." Jola thought for a moment, then nodded and gave Todor a reassuring smile—which had a similar effect on Nefeli, proud of her lover's assurance. "In which case, we'd best have a practice soon. Today, even, before the Erevestisi arrive. In two bells?"

Jola clapped, gaining Solon and Leta's attention, and gestured for them to meet her in the pavilion.

"You'll attend?" Jola asked Nefeli, with a hint of hesitation.

"Of course. As your partner, and to see how the small lot of us fare." Nefeli nodded, desire to dance with Jola warring with the million other calls on her time, then a flicker of color out on the lake drew her attention: colored sails in the distance, likely to arrive by late afternoon. "But better set the practice at one bell, as our guests will be here soon."

$\maltese$ 14 $\maltese$

Time, time, never enough time.

Jola leaned against the pavilion wall as she wrapped her sandal ties around her ankles. Her undyed, ankle-length tunic offered little warmth, leaving muscles to chill in the slightest breeze. She rolled her shoulders to loosen sinews, confident she'd warm as soon as she begun stretching. The tang of sweat from decades of dance practices hung in the air despite ample use of floral-scented cleansers.

Stout wood panels lined the circular chamber, unadorned but burnished to a warm brown. At the center of the ceiling, seven glass panels provided enough light this morning that the lanterns fastened to the walls remained unlit. The painted floor glowed with paint depicting all manner of elemental symbols, from stars to waves to flowers. That, at least, remained unchanged.

Yet with so few present, she could link every sound to a person where usually there were too many people present. This made it easier to check on the dancers' welfare—and more likely she'd get caught doing so.

The squeak over on the left near the doorway came from Solon adjusting the ties of his dancing sandals. He'd opted for an older style tunic, looped over one shoulder rather than two, but showed no sign of cold. Indeed, when she passed near enough to see him clearly drops of sweat already beaded his forehead.

A third farther around the room, Danissa dropped to her heels with a thud. She was dressed the same as Jola, save with a corded net holding her black curls off her neck. The youngest of the princesses had shoulders almost as stiff as Jola's felt, and her arms pressed tight against her side as she faced her first taught compeer partner: Todor. Who might have noticed or missed it, too busy bouncing and stretching calves and thighs.

Ylena sat on a three-legged stool in the center, back straight and chin high. Her crutches lay on the floor beside her, and linen bandages wrapped her injured leg.

What a trio of princesses Jola had been dealt: one recovering from injury, one adjusting to a less gifted compeer, and one burning out.

She preferred the ranks of compeers, or half of them.

Two taught: Todor looking anywhere except at Ylena and Solon's regular partner Leta, her regular unflappable self, a spot of cheer in a knee-length tunic draped over her tan, angular figure.

Two born compeers full of magic, although Idan, Danissa's father and until recently her regular partner, squatted next to Ylena showing less than his usual energy as he worked with Ylena through stretches for arms and upper body.

And Nefeli, smooth and graceful as always. Her lightweight dance tunic suited her, revealing her strength and solidity. A true partner, gifted, kind forgiving . . . and magical. Nefeli could tell how everyone was doing by the way they stood or sat.

Jola had to guess.

Or forge ahead and trust them to let her know if she pushed too hard.

Jola completed her usual cycle of warm-up exercises, and a sigh escaped her. Nefeli, passing near, squeezed her shoulder. Warm fingers and a gentle caress on Jola's loosening muscles.

Still loving, still supportive, suited in every way to rule. Jola rejoiced that her partner's parents had finally seen her worth to follow them.

Except, she'd follow her father not her mother. Today, at least, and for however long Jola could remain at Nefeli's side, she stood in the Terparchon's place and the Terparchon led dances—never the Marchon.

They had no music—the room was too silent save for floorboards squeaking under the shifting weight of the dancers. Jola hissed at the lack. She'd forgotten to choose from those musicians who'd played for previous practices or Dances. No time now to wait for them. She'd seen the cluster of scribes, guards, and ministers waiting outside the pavilion to fall on Nefeli as soon as practice ended.

They would just have to count, or ask Ylena or Idan to keep a beat.

But the lack of music turned out to be the least of problems plaguing the practice.

Danissa had issues adjusting to dancing with a taught compeer. Gifted though Todor was, he couldn't even hope to match a born compeer's ability to support a princess where and when she needed him. He was always a beat or two behind, which made her slow as she kept adjusting to him rather than the other way around.

This worried her father. Idan's gaze strayed regularly to Danissa and Todor, unsettling Todor to the point he as often glanced at Idan to see how he was doing, further undermining his ability to match his new princess.

Meanwhile Ylena explored what movements she can do seated. She varied between rolling her arms, weaving her hands, clapping, arching her back, and more—all of which Idan managed to match and support even with his attention split, which seemed to annoy Ylena and make her try ever more convoluted combinations.

Solon and Leta should be okay, as an experienced pair used to dancing together. Yet Solon sweated so much the floor began to grow slick where he passed. He blinked and barely focused on Jola when she told him to take a break. A moment later, he headed to the side and dropped onto a bench with his head drooped and a cloth to wipe down dangling from his hands.

A drop of Jola's own sweat trickled down to her lips, sour and salty.

"He'll settle down with a bit more to adjust." Leta rubbed her palms against her tunic. "He's just a bit nervy at the moment."

"Are you sure?" Jola asked, Nefeli a reassuring presence hovering a few steps back and clearly supporting Jola's lead.

"He has in the past." Leta frowned and glanced at him, voice dropping.

"This isn't then, this is now." Jola said.

Leta sighed, lips twisting to the side as she failed to meet Jola's gaze. "He wants this so much."

Clearly she suspected, if not knew, that Solon was heading the wrong way.

"Wanting and doing are different things." Jola shook her head. "There's much to be said for familiarity, but let's mix things all up and see if that helps."

"You want to swap partners?" Nefeli joined Jola and Leta, their three limber bodies heating the air around them.

"Yes." The last thing Jola wanted was to give up the comfort of Nefeli's partnership, but every princess knew the Dance came first. "Ease him, if you can, and see how much he can be relied upon."

But now Jola faced the same situation as Danissa, adapting to partnering with a taught compeer. Leta, whom she trusted but nowhere near the same degree as Nefeli. Jola, too, checked constantly to see where Leta was, adjusting the fall of her arm and the angle of her back and not reaching as far as when she knew Nefeli would catch and balance her.

And all the while, a faint buzzing stirred beneath her feet. The chamber where they Danced down storms lay directly below the practice pavilion. It seethed with power, enclosed within the embrace of the earth. Jola had felt the upward press of that energy before, not often but particularly at the first practice back after a long Dance, even if days later.

Never quite like this. Uneven. Starting and stopping, then surging.

No one matched evenly, and the power reflected that.

"Enough!" Jola ended practice. "It wasn't what we wanted, but the first try never is. We'll have another go tomorrow."

She waited as the others departed. Danissa and Idan, daughter and father, side-by-side. Leta and Solon helping Ylena get steady on her crutches, then pacing her as she grimly kept her injured leg off the ground. Todor farther behind, but also watching and caring.

Nefeli lingered the longest, though they both knew she could little afford it. "Solon's burning out."

"Yes. Now?" Jola wiped sweat from her forehead with the back of a hand.

Nefeli pursed her lips. "Soon. He might do better with music, as he seemed to be moving as much to the beat in his head as the one you set."

"I'll make sure to have a drummer or two tomorrow." Jola swallowed, then smiled at Nefeli. "Go, you know you're needed. I'll be behind you directly, ready to welcome the envoys."

"You're certain?" Nefeli glanced around, frowning. "There's something in the air."

Or in the wood beneath their feet, which still pulsed with an uneven beat.

"I need to douse the embers we've raised." Jola bent to touch the floor. Cool as the lake, and with a similar feel of ripples passing through. Less and less each time, or so it seemed.

"I can—" but Nefeli could not spare the time. Two of the most dedicated servants hovered in the doorway clearly anxious to get her attention. Nevertheless, she spared a few breaths to lean down and caress Jola's cheek. "Leave it, if you need. The night's cool should settle this."

Or would it?

Jola hoped so, but as she rose to take her own leave, longing for a lounge in the steam room and clean clothes, magic started rising upward. At first it seemed no more than motes of dust floating in the air. Sparkling in the angled sunlight.

Multiplying.

Power surged beneath Jola. Every pulse increased the dust. Jola's eyes itched. Blinking didn't help enough. The curved walls in the distance blurred. Dizziness made her sway. Her mouth and throat turned dry. She coughed.

The glimmering dust changed color, tinging a sickly green. Sulfurous. Poisonous.

And familiar.

She'd seen this kind of thing before, earlier in the summer when a princess and her compeer, Gisela and Stevan, had danced atop the old Shadow of the Moon. They'd moved through poisoned air, as the ghastly white stone beneath their feet flamed and exuded anger, hurt, pain, and derision.

A second round of coughing had Jola bent over, but the action cleared her head.

Every movement could be part of a Dance.

How had Gisela survived the poison and heat? She'd defied it, Danced it away.

Jola's muscles jerked. All grace and smoothness fell away as she slapped at the air. Whipped her arms and lashed out with hands willing the dust and whatever ill power it carried to move away.

Her muscles ached, the first lashes clumsy and ill-coordinated. Raising her chin, she clapped a hand against her neck and then redoubled her efforts to drive the seething magic away with kicks and thrusts to the beat of her heart.

She almost had it, whirling with palms out . . .

Then she tripped and fell to hands and knees. Even that could be Dance, as her back arched and she pretended to expel the bad air from her body.

Only to have pretense become reality as she threw up, but the foulness subsided. The sour taste of bile lingered, that and the new aches in her body from the hard Dance the remaining traces of the burst of ill magic.

This was worse than the previous instance. Amara had given Jola hope that she might move in a different direction than Solon, might move to lead Dances rather than burnout, but this suggested otherwise.

Just another piece of bad news to share with Nefeli, if they could ever find the time. Jola wanted to be the partner Nefeli needed. Was her own body betraying her?

❧ 15 ❧

How could something feel so right and so wrong in the same moment?

Late summer sunlight slanted across the wide court-yard. Sparkles flared as it bounced off circlets, necklaces and bangles. Nefeli stood at the top of a wedge-shaped staircase of gray stones washed as clean as possible. The broad facade of the palace center rose behind her, white-washed and gleaming in light or, as now, shade. She'd dressed with that in mind, her yellow tunic and mantle both heavy with gilded embroidery and a double gold circlet across her brow.

Jola at her side had, for once, chosen tunic and mantle in matching colors of orange a few shades darker than Nefeli's yellow. Her hair, piled high on her head, was still damp from the baths and left a few damp trails along the sides of her neck. Gold and silver embroidery caught the eye at neckline and hem. The air about her held a tang of cinnamon, more felt on the tongue than scented amidst the bouquet of perfumes filling the ai. Other than her circlet of twined gold and silver, she'd chosen to go without jewelry—and just as well. Even this close, Nefeli couldn't see the minute tremors rippling through her lover, but the air never stilled around her.

So right, to have Jola at her side—and yet so wrong, for Jola to show discomfort there.

Todor balanced Jola on the other side of Nefeli, silent and at ease in shades of green. Elsewise, members of the court formed a line across the top of the stairs, with Nefeli and Jola at the center, then angled down to the base. The order was ceremonial, based on a subtle combination of length of service and rank but with allowance for personal needs such as guaranteed shade or the ability to lean against a wall or sit on a bench. So many people, so many feet pressing against the ground in anxious anticipation.

No two dressed alike, making the stairs a riot of color and glitter. Such a glorious mixed-up rainbow of a sight. Other than the central building, floors and walls bore mosaics in all manner of colors. Impossibly tall people in white, red, black, and brown played at sports or war across the walls. They threw discs, ran, leapt—and danced. The floor of the courtyard matched them for splendor, featuring fish of all sizes, shapes, and colors swimming in an immense ocean of blues and grees.

When Nefeli's grandmother ruled, she'd gloried in pomp and panoply. She'd decree a color or other theme for a gathering, and woe betide anyone who failed to follow the order or stood out in anyway. *That* was for Nefeli's grandmother.

Good riddance.

Yet now Nefeli stood almost in the exact spot as her grandmother had. The Terparchon who'd had the palace built, some six or seven generations back, had indulged in a single mosaic on the top of the stairs: two sets of gold-toned footprints. One for herself at the very center, the spot best suited for display and visibility, and a second set for her consort slightly behind. Where Nefeli's grandmother had always placed herself atop the prints, Nefeli shifted slightly to the side with Jola even with her rather than behind.

Nefeli would being as she meant to go on. As a child she'd pretended a little, until her grandmother caught her at it and gave her a sharp rap on the ear. *"Compeers weren't made to rule."* The monarch's nose had twitched as though she'd smelled something sour. Even after all the years, easy to recall. Nefeli had continued to pretend in private a little longer, then stopped, not least when her powers flared and she realized how much her grandmother ruled by fear. How much her mother feared the old woman.

How hard her mother worked to be different. Her struggle to accept the need to overthrow the ruler. Her desperate desire after to give back the wealth and power the previous rulers had hoarded.

Nefeli would never be her mother, but she preferred to follow in *her* shoes.

Still, standing at the center with all eyes darting between her and the open gate, even serving as substitute ruler was overwhelming.

Somewhere in the crowd, someone watched Nefeli at every moment. Her littlest breath or movement could have long ramifications.

She licked lips suddenly dry despite the humid late afternoon air. No time to dwell on such matters.

The Erevestisi were coming. Denizens of a city that had long ignored Codaros, secure in their defensible location across the lake. Codaros encompassed more than a handful of cities of equal or greater size, and boasted an immense army Nefeli's parents still worked to shrink to a manageable size, but had never had much of a navy. Trade was conducted, often through intermediaries. Some from each land visited the other, but without official imprimatur or protections.

And now they were visiting.

A glance to either side, as subtle as Nefeli could manage, confirmed that local experts in Erevestis and its people, inasmuch as there were any, stood nearby ready to offer assistance.

But Nefeli and Jola served as hosts. On them would fall the weight of any success or failure.

The visitors were in sight, but taking their time walking from the harbor up to the palace.

The air between Nefeli and Jola vibrated all the more with the wait.

"They're here sooner than I'd expected." Nefeli hoped the simple observation might help ease Jola's tension. Distract her. "I hadn't realized they'd sail up and over instead of heading downriver and taking the bridge, then coming back up."

"Faster, and easier. Less walking." Jola swallowed, the quaver in her voice becoming less noticeable. "I wish we could sail back north to Tharis and the winter palace, rather than walking the endless roads."

Nefeli nodded. Anyone who'd endured the winding, dusty roads to make the trek between summer and winter palaces once—much less twice every year—would understand. If only there weren't so many falls on the river feeding into the lake from the north.

A rustle through the crowd, notable as it stared close to the gates and flickered inward as face after face turned so all looked in the same direction.

The guards filling the gate stepped aside and the Erevestisi entered.

Their feet felt much the same as the court gathered to welcome them—anticipation, eagerness, and a hint of worry or wariness. Impossible for Nefeli to read more in such a crowd without draining herself, or neglecting her duties as chief welcomer. Just as well, since deeper reading would be neither polite nor courteous under the circumstances.

Every report said they resembled the peoples of Codaros. Erevestis was old enough and had a long history of active trading, with the result that they'd mingled and born offspring with all manner of peoples and had the same mix of dark to light skin, hair, and eyes.

Although, Nefeli couldn't verify any of that at the moment, because their manner of dress differed so dramatically.

Nefeli and her court each wore a tunic and mantle plus varied jewelry. Perhaps the envoys also had jewelry, but it was impossible to tell. Each and every one wore layered robes of nearly transparent gauze in a myriad of colors, and sashed at the waist with chains or braided strips of cloth. The robes covered them from throat to ankles, but were dagged or gashed along the sleeves and skirts to reveal the layers below. Each had a different combination of colors.

"What do the colors mean?" Nefeli asked, just loud enough to reach her advisors over the steady tromp of the visitor's sandals and boots.

The chief librarian perched on a bench behind her hissed. His assistant coughed. "Hard to tell at this distance," she said. "There are so many subtleties that I've never managed to figure out. But look for the person with the most colors, they'll be the highest in rank or importance."

That proved harder to figure out from a distance than Nefeli would have thought. The layers of sleeves and skirts fluttered around them as they moved, defying easy counting.

Worse, everyone had one or more additional layers of gauze covering their heads and blurring their features. Even as they drew close and and began to climb the stairs, the veils allowed the watchers only hints of what they looked like beneath.

The visitors' guards stood out from the others, because their robes ended above the ankle and they wore boots rather than sandals. They'd surrendered their swords at the gate, but retained long daggers. Yet even they covered their hair and faces.

Sudden discomfort rippled through the crowd in an uneven progression from various points as one then seven then twice or three times as many passed on the realization that the Erevestisi walked mostly in pairs. They evidently favored even numbers—considered more likely to bring bad luck in Codaros, but evidently not in Erevestis —although overall there were an odd number of them. Fourteen guards and seven envoys.

Yet who led?

"Look to the center." The librarian behind Nefeli advised.

"The most colors?" Nefeli asked.

"I can't tell how many colors they have in their clothes, yet, but they're the only with a hood tinged silver instead of light blue."

"Jola, Todor, please accompany me." Nefeli drew in a deep breath and started down the stairs. She calculated her pace carefully, matching the weight of the approaching visitors' steps.

They met one-third of the way down from the top. Two guards stood behind each envoy—who arrayed themselves with three in a straight line, matching Nefeli and her companions. The four other envoys remained two steps back and spread to either side.

"Welcome to Codaros. Welcome to Yaris. Welcome to the summer palace and the court of the Terparchon." Nefeli nodded at each of the three. Blurred faces gazed back at her, tinged silver and blue. Each had at least three layers of veils in addition to the eight or nine, or more, colors of their robes. The veils made finding differences between them difficult, especially in the angled afternoon light. The air around vibrated as neither Jola nor Todor managed to remain completely still. Neither could Nefeli, for that matter.

Much as Nefeli wanted to bring them inside, to have them settle on couches and speak face to face, or face to hood, ceremony bound her. This was the first meeting, and it had to take place in the open where all might hear and listen. She spoke slow and clear as she introduced herself, Jola, and Todor.

The veils and light concealed any reaction from the envoys, though they'd been warned in advance that they wouldn't meet the Terparchon or Marchon in person.

"We accept your welcome, Nefeli daughter of Chloris, speaker for the Terparchon." The envoy to the left had a low-pitched voice that echoed along the stairs and walls despite the crowd. The words slid into each other as though connected with almost-but-not-quite aspirated esses.

"We greet princess Jola, of whom praise has spread far, and compeer Todor, son of Chloris." With scarce time for the first to breathe, the envoy to the right took up in their place. They had a much higher voice, almost as resonant—but with the same slurring accent.

"We bring all good wishes for health and happiness from the Council of Erevestis to their co-equals of other lands." The deeper-voiced envoy said.

"We may speak of many things, but be aware we speak for ourselves and not the Council." For a third time, the transition between the two took less than a breath.

"We accept your possibilities and limitations." Nefeli stretched hands out to either side. "Please come in, and let us speak in comfort as we break bread and share water."

"We thank you." The higher-voices said.

"We accept your offer," said the lower a moment after.

Again the play between the two. Nefeli nodded to each, then turned and ascended. She caught Jola and Todor's gaze as she passed, for they would wait and follow behind the three lead envoys.

If only Nefeli's mother had appointed both Nefeli and Jola to stand in her and the Marchon's stead rather than Nefeli alone. Then Nefeli could share the weight and responsibility—but hers was the fault, in part, for not having asked.

The gulf between them seemed wider filled by these strangers.

The two envoys who seemed appointed to speak took turns responding to Nefeli's queries about their trip, and asking questions in turn. They answered everything alternative back and forth. As they passed through the halls, the lights affixed to the walls occasionally offered hints of the features blurred beneath their hoods—coiled curls at the lower-voiced's nape, and a hint of beard growth on the chin of the higher.

The need to glance constantly between them, and the steady predictability of their taking turns left Nefeli on edge by the time they reached the wide reception hall. A mosaic of a previous Terparchon raising the palace covered the floor. Wide windows set into thick walls opened onto gardens redolent of greenery and sweet pine smells. The room faced north, and caught just enough of the late summer setting sun to give the walls a faint orange tinge. Paired couches covered in blues and greens formed a loose circle, separated by round tables bearing trays of cool drinks and savory treats.

No couch stood out, all equal. Nefeli waved a hand as the other envoys and a similar number of courtiers entered. The Erevestisi guards and an equal number of Codaros' plus one interfiled to line the walls.

The two speaking envoys exchanged glances through their hoods, heads turning to face each other by the angle of fabric over noses. They continued the alternating patter as they declined the honor of choosing a seat first and begged the privilege of being placed where Nefeli preferred.

Before Nefeli could untangle the headache of deciding where they should go, much less telling them so, the silver-veiled raised her hands. Nefeli found it difficult to count the number of colors anyone wore when it went above three. Despite the dags and slashes, the thin tunics overlapped leaving it unclear whether orange was a separate color or close layers of yellow and red.

Nevertheless, this one clearly wore well over a half-dozen colors, perhaps even a dozen.

"Enough." No hint of an ess in the word, though a hint of a rasp underscored the eff-sound lingered on at the end.

A clear order. The other two quieted, heads bowing.

The leader removed two of their veils, handing one to each of the envoys who'd spoken. One hissed, fingers trembling as they took the cloth, but said nothing.

The single layer remaining was fine and almost translucent. Only a faint blurring marred dark eyes amid a sharp-featured and dark-complected face with a suggestion of wrinkles. Silver threaded through dark hair braided and coiled around their head.

They studied Nefeli even as she did them.

"You have a little resemblance to your grandfather." They had only a hint of the others' accent, sounding much closer to the crisper tones Nefeli was accustomed to in the court and Yaris.

But the words and sentiment . . . Nefeli stiffened. The Erevestisi didn't specify which of Nefeli's grandfathers they meant, though it didn't much matter as both had died before Nefeli's birth. Before Nefeli's parents met and married for that matter. Still, the other offered much in a few words—indicating a past marked by travel far. She waved to a couch and headed to the one closest to it. "You do me honor."

"No honor, though truth I mean no discourtesy either." The envoy settled where Nefeli indicated, but sat with sandals flat on the floor rather than reclining. Nefeli mirrored her posture. "It is merely an observation."

A nod at the other envoys, and they spaced themselves around the room as Jola and Todor and other princesses and compeers filed in between them. No one else spoke, nor even gestured at the drinks and food awaiting. The hush allowed every word to fill the room.

"I mean your mother's father," the envoy said as all sat and the hush fell. "For I knew him briefly when I wandered, many years ago, and stopped in Tharis long enough to see the stars among other matters. I am Cahide of Erevestis. I have no title, though some have called me lady out of respect, nor do I claim any place of power or influence on the Council save that there are those upon it who hold a certain respect for me."

Trading phrases as before, the other two envoys leapt in to add that the Council held more than respect for Cahide. She was counted among the wise, for few others had traveled so widely or learned as much.

Cahide's smile was wide enough to make the single veil twitch slightly. She nodded at each in turn.

Still, this close, the slight twitch to the stranger's toes betrayed some degree of nervousness.

No doubt she could see the same on Nefeli's feet.

"I do not wish to raise false hopes, nor pretend to that which I am not. I bring no promises, no gold, no trade alliances," Cahide said. "But the Shadows of the Moon have been an especial interest of mine all my years, and I have heard of the change here. Of the Shadow gone."

"So I have been told, and we will be pleased to escort you there tomorrow." Nefeli pressed a jittery hand against her chest. "At first light if you wish."

"A little later will be acceptable, too, as you chose." Cahide sighed and smiled more broadly, toes still twitching. "I would ask to be permitted to at least one visit at night, when the flowers glow and whisper. For most particularly I wish to pay my respects to those buried beneath it and, now that the Shadow hiding their loss is gone, if the flowers consent, learn their names and fates."

Nefeli froze. The former Shadow was a grave? Shock rippled through the court and visitors. Evidently Cahide had not told her fellow envoys all of what she wanted, though they'd known some part; the Erevestisi guards, however, hadn't heard though their only sign of surprise was stiffened postures.

But astonishment marked every one of the Codaros courtiers and guards.

With one exception. One couch over from Nefeli, on the other side of the lower-voiced envoy, Jola sat straight and still—but her lack of movement and expression differed from the rest.

Evidently Jola hadn't told Nefeli something else. How many more secrets lay between them?

16

Jola caught the shift in Nefeli's posture. She sat near enough to her lover that she couldn't miss the sudden stiffness of Nefeli's shoulders, and press of upper arms against her side. Others might not realize, hopefully did not, but Jola's long familiarity with Nefeli permitted her some degree of insight no matter that she lacked her lover's gift.

Jola's head and back ached from the dance practice, and the failure after. The single roll she'd managed to sneak before the envoy's arrival sat heavy in her belly. The couch beneath Jola suddenly seemed softer, as though sucking her down and pinning her in place. Shifting her feet against the tiled floor, she tightened her thighs and straightened further. Ten years of dancing and court life had given her ample practice at keeping her head high and expression open.

Hiding one's feelings at court wasn't required. The Terparchon and Marchon appreciated honest reactions—but they preferred thoughtful responses. Jola had struggled at first, until one of her mother's advised her to consider it as similar to cooking. Some ingredients and recipes called for a quick dip in boiling water, or a fast fix in the baking oven. Others required longer to simmer or stew. Somehow, the notion had helped Jola develop a calm demeanor and the tucking of matters away to ponder and decide later.

After all, she was very good at pondering. It ranked akin to worrying, at which she also excelled.

No one showed any sign of noticing Jola's distraction, not the strangers, not the guards, and not even her fellow princesses and compeers. The rest were one and all still reacting to Cahide's question about bodies under the former Shadow.

Only Nefeli caught it.

With Nefeli's keen intelligence and perception, even if she didn't use her compeer magic, she'd have noticed Jola's reaction. Connected it to Cahide's question. Added Jola's earlier brief confession—and come up with details missing.

If only Cahide hadn't asked, which would've required her not to come, or any of the envoys since it seemed her interests drove the mission—as well as for night not to fall. One moment Jola gritted her teeth and stuffed down a glare at the unwitting envoy, then let resentment go.

The visitor wasn't the problem. Indeed, she might even be able to explain the events of the night should Jola ever risk sharing them.

No, Jola's problem was her own doing. Anyone who kept secrets ought to prepare for them to escape, one way or another. She shouldn't have agreed with the others to make the events secret, or required an exception for Nefeli.

Too late now. Known or unknown, secrets divided people and mixed up priorities.

Yet Nefeli surmounted all personal qualms to offer Cahide and the other envoys only a warm welcome.

"I look forward to discussing the Shadows and their lore with you, but perhaps later?" Nefeli gestured at the windows and the ruddy evening light glowing on the garden landscape. "For tonight, we have planned a small reception and dinner, and tomorrow morning we will take you to the former Shadow with time to study, mourn, or what you will."

Jola hovered behind, helping to match envoys and guards to servants who would take them to their quarters. Answering a few questions from courtiers. Always, she positioned herself where she could watch Nefeli out of the corner of her eye.

A dullness fell upon Jola, wrapping her tight. No fear or worry pierced it. Blood pounded in her veins and at her temples as she waited for a hand to settle on her arm. Warmth flared through the layers of Jola's tunic and mantle, but no surprise.

"Come." Nefeli neither pushed nor pulled, but Jola followed where she went. "Let us rest before the evening's entertainment."

They walked in silence through the corridors as the rest of the court dispersed. With guards accompanying them, it was neither the time or place for confrontation or discussion. The familiar walls were merely colored blurs passed in certain order until they reached Nefeli's rooms.

No, Nefeli and Jola's rooms.

For now.

The door shut behind Jola. She leaned back against it for a moment, not-quite trembling though perhaps her fingertips rattled against the firm wood. Drawing in a deep breath and pressing an unsteady hand against her belly, she followed in Nefeli's wake.

Her lover crossed the room and positioned herself at the far edge of a wide window gazing off into the distance. Jola couldn't make out what Nefeli saw—it was all a blur of green and gray shadows to her— but given the angle Nefeli just might be able to see where the former Shadow lay. Or near to it.

A drop of perspiration trickled down Jola's cheek. She wiped her face with the back of a hand.

"You left out details earlier, when you finally told me." Nefeli leaned against the window frame, arms crossed and head tilted to the far side. A wisp of wind tugged at a curl come loose from her high-piled hair. "Late. In a hurry. In public."

Jola swallowed her first reaction, a desperate urge to plea for forgiveness. After a few breaths, she clasped her hands and angled herself to face her lover. "I'm sorry."

"So you said." Nefeli's gaze remained fixed on something in the distance.

"I didn't realize that sharing the secret with the others who were there but not with you would make distance between us." A hiss escaped Jola, of disappointment at her lack of forethought. "Or that it would come to hurt you now."

"I believe you." Such a calm, quiet reply. If only Nefeli would look at Jola.

And Jola took Nefeli's words for truth, but they brought no pleasure—only more disappointment and a deep, gut-clenching certainty that this was the end.

So many times Jola had envisioned what might happen to part them. Injury or inability to dance on Jola's part—her body failing her in some way—usually ranked high, with Nefeli being inevitably kind and considerate as Jola left court. Or Nefeli falling for someone else and refusing to follow her heart until dealing honestly with Jola.

So many painful possibilities considered. Expected. Braced against, in hopes that the pain would be less that way.

Instead, an impulsive act undid all Jola held most dear. She'd disappointed the woman she loved, by placing others between them. No matter that Jola had done so in a moment of fear, she'd still chosen to have a secret with them rather than be honest with her lover.

Swallowing hard, she lowered her head until her line of sight dwindled to her dusty sandaled feet and the orange hem of her swaying tunic. Braced herself for dismissal. Polite and kind, of course, with care to ensure the break didn't impact court, but still dismissal.

Yet very different words fell on her ears instead.

"Why didn't you trust me?" Nefeli asked.

Jola shook her head. The movement made her dizzy, and she stumbled over to drop on the nearest couch. The one Nefeli preferred, cushions squeaking under her.

So much practicing, so many expectations of the worst—but it hadn't materialized.

What was Jola thinking? Would she give up without taking a stand? She licked lips gone dry and raised her head.

Nefeli hadn't moved, still gazing off into the distance. Still, her shoulders were slumped and arms crossed over her chest.

"It's not you—" Jola started.

"If you trusted me you'd have shared *something*, and earlier." Nefeli finally turned to face Jola. The distance was just short enough to make the tic jittering in her cheek unmistakable.

"It's your mother I fear." Jola grabbed a pitcher from the table between the couches. Three-quarters full with lukewarm water, any ice having melted, but better than nothing. She filled a mug and drained it.

"I'm not her. Can't you tell the difference?"

"It was instinct." Jola refilled the mug and drank deep again. Swallowed explanations that wouldn't ease the hurt. "I was wrong. I'm sorry."

"Very well." Nefeli settled on the opposite couch, drawing her feet up under her. She shook her head refusing water when Jola offered.

"May I tell you the whole now?" Jola asked.

"You didn't earlier?"

Jola swallowed rather than return the bitterness or sarcasm. She rubbed her hands, fingers cool against her palms. "You have all the main pieces, but . . . I trust myself to you, but this means also trusting you not to act against the others because I'm breaking my word to them."

"I make no promises. You'll have to choose how much to trust me."

A choice, a chance. Jola settled into the cushions, glad they were slightly uncomfortable and more shaped to Nefeli's body than hers.

"It started after that big storm." She'd start at the beginning. "I came out of the baths after the Dance late at night, one of the last. Tere was damage to the palace, though not much. Never much."

Her lips tightened briefly. A small grunt escaped Nefeli. They'd talked more than once over their last years about the extent to which Nefeli's mother sometimes seemed as much or more bent on protecting the summer and winter palaces when easing storms or other disasters as caring for the cities and the general populace. More than once Jola's family had to deal with ice dams and flooding while the winter palace came through without notable damage.

Nefeli had explained that her mother considered the palaces symbols of the princesses' ability to care for the land and people. They'd agreed to disagree.

"Gisela was there, and Danissa, both staring at something, the mosaic I think, but I'm not sure." Jola blinked, thinking back to that night. "All of a sudden Gisela stormed off into the woods, though she was still a newcomer, barely at court more than a quarter-moon. She hardly knew her way around!" The new princess might be older than Jola, but it had been quite clear she'd never lived anywhere as big and complex as court. "So we followed her, Danissa and I did, and she went right to the Shadow. Stomped over to it and started Dancing."

Memories wrapped around Jola—even as sullen power had seeped from the sickly white stones and turned to a poisonous green grass. The air turned hot and hard to breathe for Jola, several lengths away, and how much worse must it have been for Gisela as she realized the Shadow could—would—kill her.

The couch rocked as Nefeli settled next to Jola. She wrapped warm hands around Jola's fingers—not the same as holding Jola, but something. The closeness made it easier to try and put the night into words.

"Gisela called for help, said she needed Stevan. Danissa ran to get him, leaving me there. I couldn't do anything, there was no dance that could help, and I was only one princess. I didn't know, then that princesses could work great magic alone. I had to watch Gisela turn a sickly green-white." Jola leaned against Nefeli, shoulder to shoulder. "Stevan came, sooner than I'd have thought, with Brenn behind him. Stevan and Gisela Danced. I've never seen such power in a princess and compeer, never. Until at last, he lifted her high and she somehow summoned a bolt of lightning. They leapt free and it struck the Shadow. That much was true of all the stories."

She turned to meet Nefeli's gaze, faces only a breath apart.

Nefeli nodded, lips pursed and eyes narrowed. "And the bodies?" she asked.

"There were two, where the Shadow had been." Jola waved a hand. "The lightning revealed them. Winds lifted them up and they turned to dust and blew away. Then the flowers came."

"Anything else?"

"No. That's all, though it's hard to describe the poison air or the dance magic or . . ." Jola stung her feet onto the floor and sat slumped on the couch.

"And you witnessed this all." One of Nefeli's hands traced a line along Jola's arm to her shoulder, leaving tingles where her fingers passed.

"Watched only. I did nothing, didn't help Gisela, or summon Stevan," Jola said. "We were worried about them, with both being so new, that the Terparchon would throw them out of court or worse. Maybe the rest of us, too. And it didn't seem so bad, trading the horrid Shadow for flowers." Her voice trailed off and her cheeks heated.

"I cannot fault you for being loyal to those you care for, even if it came at my expense." Nefeli sighed.

But hurt shone on her face.

"I could have pushed to share with you, and no one else. To have asked you to keep it secret," Jola shrugged. "But then I'd be asking you to keep it from your mother."

"It wouldn't be the first time I'd done that." Nefeli turned to match Jola's posture, hip to hip and shoulder to shoulder.

A hint of chill tinged the air as the sky turned blazing colors. The sun had half-set. They had only a little longer before they'd need to change and head to dinner. Savory flavorings already floated on the wind up from the kitchens.

"Look at me." Nefeli said.

Not a command, but neither something Jola would refuse. She turned, searching her lover's face for reason to hope.

Found a gentle smile tinged with regret, but love shining in those glorious brown eyes.

"I forgive you for this." Nefeli took Jola's hands. "But it must not happen again. We have to stand together if we're to rule. My parents live at a distance from each other. Keep secrets, make their own alliances even as they also work together—but that's not what I want. I want a partner beside me, hand in hand to face all things together. Someone willing to be with me despite the costs because they care for me. I want you to be that person, but only if you want it too."

Amidst all the fearful dreaming of Nefeli dismissing her, Jola had squeezed daydreams of declarations of love as well. Poetic and grand, but nothing approaching the honesty and heart she'd been given.

"Oh, I do." Jola pulled her hands free to wrap Nefeli in a close embrace and bury her suddenly tear-damp face against her lover's shoulder.

For a few long breaths, she indulged in the perfection of the moment.

Then her sore back muscles twanged under the press of Nefeli's hands. Muscles strained trying to contain power earlier that day. Given all that had passed between them, Jola couldn't keep quiet.

"Except, I have to warn you that I may not be able to be what you want."

"Of course you can. You're a great leader and princess." Nefeli cupped Jola's cheek, then concern flared across her face. "Don't you believe in yourself? I do."

"It's not a matter of belief in myself. Rather, I may be burning out as a princess."

17

"**B**urning out."

Nefeli rubbed her forehead, bracelets jingling around her wrist. Her body had dropped from a warm embrace to the chill of distance too fast. Her arms were empty, her lover retreated to the far end of the couch. Jola's wrinkled mantle had slipped from one shoulder, but she didn't seem to notice.

Nefeli's beloved princess's head bowed low, shoulders drawn in.

A bell rang in the distance, warning of time passing—but this had priority.

"I've had instances where magic has gone wrong around me and I've Danced without intending to do so." She held up two fingers. "The first might have been Solon's fault—he's burning out, too—but I did something odd that gathered unwanted magic and placed it on the earth. I thought—hoped—it was just him, but earlier today something else happened. There was magic loose in the practice chamber after the rest of you had gone, harsh and smoky. I tried to gather it and dance it away, but nearly crisped myself in the process. I'm not sure how I survived without being burned."

"Solon's danced twice your years. I'm not surprised by him tipping into burnout." Nefeli jerked to her feet and paced along the length of the room. "Maybe it was all him, and you were left to cleanup as the last to leave the chamber?"

"Solon's had one of the longest tenures of any princesses. We're fortunate he's only coming to the point now. Princesses rarely last a decade, and I'm at that mark. It could be, and wanting it to be all him isn't fair or true."

Nefeli shifted her pacing to extend into the bedroom and retrieve warmer tunics and mantles better suited to the evening festivities. She laid Jola's on the sofa next to her lover, then retreated a few lengths back to start changing. Her fingers fumbled with the lines of the fabric, nearly ripping her mantle as she doffed it. "Compeers rarely last five years. Dance is hard on all of us."

"Taught compeers, yes, but born compeers such as you and Idan may dance for all your lives." The soft swish of silk underscored Jola's words as she slipped from her clothes.

"Idan has." He was an example Nefeli hoped to live up to, having Danced near his whole life. "But there were other born compeers who burned out, or were injured or died young."

"Still, just because compeers also burn out does not make princesses burning out less of a problem. Or our losses less important. Or frightening." Despite having started after, Jola finished shifting into a turquoise tunic and deep purple mantle, both liberally edged in gold and silver. She practically glowed, her earlier clothes a pile of orange at her feet.

"I didn't—" Nefeli draped her own purple mantle, trimmed only in gold, over a black tunic.

"You will remain here at court in a place of importance whether or not you Dance." Jola shook her head. "But the rest of us are well aware that when we can no longer Dance we dwindle in importance to the court. Some few manage to keep high position, most leave, sooner or later."

"Not you." Nefeli grabbed Jola's hands and squeezed. "I want you at my side."

"That's what I want, too." Jola squeezed back, dampness glittering at the corners of her eyes. "But I have Danced for a decade—and now my dancing is changing. It may be that I am developing the ability to direct other princesses in Dancing, as your mother does. Amara said that might be. But it is also possible that I am burning out. That magic will escape me and turn to fire or water, and I the cause of the kind of damage and loss that princesses seek to prevent. I don't know. Only that earlier today, I nearly burned to a crisp."

Nefeli pulled Jola in close, holding her tight. With their heads pressed this close, a hint of burnt hair clung to Jola's head. Or was that merely fear?

Jola could have died.

Tightening the embrace, heedless of wrinkling their clothes, Nefeli rejoiced in the pulse thumping at Jola's throat, and the rise and fall of her chest.

Wished they could stay this way. Tried to hold fast as Jola pulled back. Feared what Jola might say, even as Nefeli knew Jola must say it.

"If I cannot dance, I cannot stand beside you when you are named heir to the Marchon and your partner heir to the Terparchon." Jola dabbed at tears—hers and the ones Nefeli hadn't realized she was shedding. "You will have to choose another princess to pair with."

"*If.*" Nefeli matched Jola's gaze, refusing to allow her to turn away. "I want you by my side whether or not you can become Terparchon after my mother dies."

Jola shook her head, but Nefeli only raised her chin higher.

"That is if you are burning out, which I will not believe," Nefeli said. "There's never been a hint of it in how you walk and move."

"You've read how I stand on the ground?" Jola asked.

"Only in the simplest of ways, as I promised." Nefeli's cheeks heated. She'd tried not to do more, or to track Jola often, even though it was as natural as breathing to see where her lover was at any given moment. "But it helps to know where you are when you're not with me, and that you're safe."

Jola pulled back and stretched out her arms. "Then see now – tell me what you can find."

The last golden rays of sunlight gilded her.

"You're certain." Nefeli asked.

A nod, and an extra breath to allow for second thoughts, then Nefeli unleashed her power and let it focus on Jola. Nefeli had never paid such close attention to how Jola pressed against the ground, not since first realizing her attraction to the princess and feared influencing her.

A thrum rippled through Nefeli, pulsing to the beat of Jola's heart. Her body radiated health, albeit tinged with the usual edge of exhaustion and aches that no dancer could escape.

Beneath the health lay worry. Not a surprise, for Jola always worried—it showed in an odd knot or twist in how she stood, rarely completely square and flat except when required for a Dance.

Next, Nefeli found something odd. Warm and mostly round but with flickers. Warm, not hot. No crackle and lash of flames or sullen glow of embers.

Stretching her senses through the buildings, Nefeli sought Solon, to compare the two.

The many pains pinging in his muscles and joints made her teeth ache in sympathy. He sat slumped on his bed, feet hot against the floor. No flames here, but embers certainly and a rill of added warmth spiraling through him.

In contrast, Jola seemed more self-contained. A seed, perhaps, where what was in Solon was growing.

"I can't tell." Nefeli shivered as she pulled her power back until she knew only who was within a certain proximity—unfortunately including the envoys about to leave their quarters. A layer of sweat made her tunic stick in places—or was it the absence of the warmth in Jola and heat in Solon? "You're not burning out the way Solon is, not yet. Maybe not ever. There's something different there."

Jola nodded, face open and clearly showing she slipped into worrying.

Wrapping hands around the back of Jola's head, Nefeli pressed their bodies together. She stared into her lover's eyes. "But we have time. You aren't likely to become Terparchon any time soon. Mother is well and healthy and could well live for decades more. Stay with me. There are no guarantees. I know you worry—but give us the time we have. Don't decide today what you may not have to decide tomorrow."

Jola paused, head starting to bob agreement. She opened her mouth to speak—

But a bell rang out. The dinner bell.

Nefeli stepped back and offered Jola her arm. Lips curved, Jola linked hers through it. They took a moment to brush wrinkles from each other's clothes, then headed out. Their guards fell into step behind them. Nefeli kept her head high as she strode through the halls.

She'd had a few glorious moments of knowing Jola wanted to be with her, to exult in the mutuality of their love and kick away the last fragments of Ylena's voice comparing Jola and Nefeli to Todor and her.

The sourness crept in too soon. Nefeli didn't worry, not as Jola dug into fears and held them close. No, Nefeli preferred practical consideration of problems and development of solutions.

Still, too many problems pressed—ones she couldn't, quite, push away.

Cahide had mentioned bodies buried under the Shadow, something Nefeli hadn't known of before or anyone else that she was aware of. What other secrets or little known facts might she hold close or let drop before she left?

Not a pleasant thought, but preferable to the other concerns.

A cold lump grew in Nefeli's stomach.

If Jola *did* burn out and couldn't lead Dances as Terparchon, someone else would have to but who? Would they be willing to serve as Terparchon only for Dance purposes or demand more power? As heir or as Marchon, Nefeli might have someday to chose between the love of her life and the welfare of her country—unless she could find ways to make everything balance.

A dollop of guilt matched the cold lump. Nefeli had pushed Jola to promise allegiance to Nefeli over others, to share the secret about watching the destruction of the Shadow—but there was that other secret Nefeli hadn't shared with anyone. Much, much smaller than Jola's secret, and yet . . .

❧ 18 ☙

Jola hurried through the mostly empty halls. Sandals clacked against the tiled floors, tripled thanks to the two guards tromping in her wake. Her circlet sat light atop her coiled hair, but would no doubt press much heavier by the end of the day. Jola usually wore cords to denote her rank, but hosting the envoys called for finer attire. A dark green mantle embroidered with leaves and vines kept her silky purple tunic from flapping in every breeze, save around her ankles. She'd never dance in such clothes, too ornate and heavy, but appreciated the way the fabrics accentuated movements.

A lingering stiffness troubled her shoulders and back despite careful stretches and warm-up exercises, but otherwise felt as though she walked on air. Nefeli's sweet care and encouragement made it hard not to smile. Although Nefeli had snuck out of the bed first without waking Jola, she'd left behind a deep pink flower on her pillow, which Jola had tucked behind her ear. Each and every one of the—few— members of court she met had a twinkle in their eye or nodded at the flower and smiled.

The air held a tang of autumn, a mere hint of a chill which made Jola chuckle. In the north, such a breeze would be considered balmy.

Still, out the windows the gardens had begun to turn from the extravagant rainbow array of summer flowers to the quieter golds and pinks of fall.

One by one or two by two, Jola checked on the remaining princesses and compeers—lingering long with no one. She paused to place the bells and count the strikes as the different towers rang out the passage of time. Most were fine, if tired or prickly over the changes in partnering.

Yet strangely Ylena and Solon, the two she was most concerned about, she found together in the infirmary with their heads close. Ylena sat on a chair, foot propped up on a stool. The pale-gray folds of her plain tunic and mantle emphasized her fair—and healthy —coloring.

In contrast, Solon had a grayish tinge and dark lines under his eyes, a perfect match for his dark-gray tunic. He'd wrapped a thick blue mantle around his shoulders, the tasseled ends bouncing against his knees as he huddled on a stool.

Only days ago he'd been fine, if absent-minded.

"Welcome." Ylena nodded at Jola and gave a half-wave, speaking before Jola could. "What do you want? Aren't you off to the Shadow with the Erevestisi?"

"Soon. Just wanted to see how you're doing." Jola waved at the quiet plaza. Murmurs and soft clatters in the near-distance attested that most of the infirmary staff remained at the summer palace year-round. "Better here, perhaps, since the halls are not so empty?"

"You can say that twice." Solon shivered. "It's so quiet without anyone snoring or getting in late and bumping down the hall apologizing to the doors."

"I'm fine, fine, fine." Ylena said.

"One fine would suffice." Jola settled on a bench. "Does three mean thrice as fine?"

"No, but it was good to be back in the practice hall yesterday. Awkward, as first times always go, but . . ." Ylena crossed her arms and scowled, except a hint of a smile lifted the ends of her lips. "I will have to apologize to Danissa when I next see her. She was right that I could dance without using my leg. I dislike it when other people are more right than me."

"Hmm." Solon tilted his head to the side. "She said I was dancing too tight."

"She was probably right about that, too." Ylena studied him. "And you may be over-doing things."

"Agreed. You did keep your movements close yesterday." Jola welcomed the excuse to stare at him. The angle of his shoulders and back, and the fall of the mantle, suggested stiff muscles. "Doing any better?"

"Sometimes. When I forget to think about it." He grimaced, flashing sharp teeth. "Except then I forget something *else,* and wind up adding a half-step into a glide, then I trip and magic flares. Once a day, I think I should just give up and retire now, even if I have the pay my own way home."

"You can travel with the court regardless, don't worry about that." Jola patted his shoulder. She had no fear making the promise, certain Nefeli would agree. "So dance or not as you *will*, not because you *must*. Are you warming up enough?"

"Yes, mother." Solon winced. "Except when I'm not. But some-times I can't sleep so I get up in the dead of night to stretch. Then when I do rest, I dream and voices in my head keep reminding me to go on so I can end in a big blaze."

"Ah." Jola exchanged glances with Ylena, unsure how to respond, then patted him again. "Well, when we're back in Tharis for winter, a warm fire will be nice."

"You're too nice." Ylena said, laying a hand on Solon's arm. "Go escort the Erevestisi and leave us alone to be grumpy together."

Jola preferred to remain, and ask Solon more about his experience of burning out—though not in front of Ylena. The bells rang out, marking the time, and she left instead.

A shortcut through a kitchen garden, where gardeners picked berries and starmeg for storing or supper, and Jola met the others at the grand plaza overlooking the lake. All but two of the envoys were present, with their guards. The brisk breeze tugged at their many layers, flipping bits of cloth this way and that. The guards wore shades of the same color, mostly reds and blues with one in green. The envoys remained in a motley array of colors that contrasted or complemented in no understandable pattern.

Maybe they wore what colors they liked, as Jola did. She smiled, liking the idea even though she knew there were patterns she just lacked the knowledge to decipher them. Likewise the number and arrangement of the veils. Cahide wore one veil, silver, but the others still had two or three obscuring their features.

Nefeli had chosen to keep the numbers small for the visit—first or only, it wasn't clear how much or often the visitors would want to retrace their steps. Still, she was there and Todor and Jola, along with their guards, and Cahide and four other envoys and their guards. It added up.

But the best route to the site lay along a narrow path through woods thick enough that they formed a long, thin entourage. The leafy cover allowed ample light through while providing shade that made Jola thankful for her heavier mantle.

Jola wound up escorting Cahide. The visitor had so deftly deflected the honor of walking with Nefeli onto her fellow envoys that neither Nefeli nor Jola had responded in time to prevent the arrangement.

The elder walked slower than the other envoys. Jola matched her pace, watching Nefeli forge ahead at a more rapid rate. Behind them, the last of the guards—a mix of visitors and Codaros—left room between.

Voices and the thumps of sandals and boots carried, but mingled with sweet toots and coos as brightly plumaged songbirds darted about. It was possible to hear what others before or behind said, but one had to pay close attention.

Jola did not dare do so, given her companion.

They moved in near silence at first, as the Erevestisi adjusted to the mix of stepping stones and hard earth. She rested a hand on Jola's arm, but barely needed it for balance.

Jola had time to almost count the number of different colors in Cahide's layers—stopping at nine or ten when the other finally spoke.

"Princess Jola, I did not have an opportunity yesterday to express what a pleasure it is to meet you." Cahide said. "I have heard so much about you."

"Indeed?" Jola blinked, as startled at that as by the yellow-tailed songbird passing nearly a hands' breadth in front. "I hadn't realized word of me spread. I'm but one of twelve princesses attending on the Terparchon."

"Hardly but one." The envoy clicked her tongue. "It is you, is it not, who set up schools to teach and trade dance instruction in every city in your land?"

"Some, yes, mostly the largest cities."

"But smaller as well."

"Instructors who relocate, not many but some, often ask for permission to start schools where they go, but I have not visited all." Jola glanced at her companion, perplexed by the warm approval clear through the single veil.

"And your schools employ many retired princesses and compeers, plus other dancers, and organize fetes and opportunities for revelry and artistry." Cahide gripped Jola slightly tighter as they eased down a narrow, angled stretch.

"Some yes."

"Yet you think word of your accomplishments would not spread? To the contrary, many of my correspondents, and I have traveled enough that I rejoice in contacts throughout the continent, have mentioned you and how your schools undo mysteries of movement and encourage people to share and explore different manner of dances." Cahide's voice rose, enough to carry across the distance between them and the three in front of them. "I say again, it is a pleasure to meet you and find you so well situated."

Nefeli glanced back, smiling and nodding at both.

Warmth spread through Jola as their gazes met, and lingered even when Nefeli returned her attention to her two walking companions.

Nefeli had forgiven Jola for keeping secrets, and still wanted them side by side into a future increasingly rosy. The royal compeer had finally said all the words Jola had longed for years to hear.

One way or another, Jola would live up to Nefeli's trust.

As Cahide continued to discuss Jola's network of dance instruction and exchanges, her admiration sank in. It was an accomplishment. Not Jola's alone, of course, for she would be nowhere without the many retired princesses and compeers, and others, who held everything together day by day. Nevertheless, without Jola there to advocate for them at court, to weave them into a whole, and ensure contact and exchanges between cities, it might well have wilted on the vine.

Although Jola had doubted her place with Nefeli, and her potential to lead Dances, she'd never doubted she could learn what she needed to take on many of the Terparchon's non-magical duties. The complications of moving court, keeping peace between the cities, ensuring sharing of resources . . . they were variations on things Jola had already done.

And she wouldn't have to tackle any of it alone—she'd work alongside Nefeli, hand-in-hand.

Jola just had to find a way to avoid burnout.

Nefeli had visited the Shadow at least once or thrice a summer every year of her life. Every aspect was familiar in one way or another. She might even have been able to walk there, around, and back blindfolded, though she'd never put that to the test. Since the great change, she'd paid several more visits—first with Jola, then without.

Yet every time she'd come since the change, she noticed something new. The newness began this trip even before they reached the edge of the woods. The trees still crowded around, and a flair of seven song-birds in varying shades of yellow and blue whipped around a tree ahead. The bird population had increased in mere weeks. Last time she'd seen few to none.

A breeze curling along the path wafted a sweet perfume. Light and airy, it defied description—and lured one forward. Light beckoned where the trees gave way to a wide clearing. As soon as Nefeli reached the edge, she stepped aside onto one of the flat stones ringing the circular opening. Another path led straight almost to the center before splitting into a smaller circle around what had once been a ghastly white expanse of stones.

The low-growing grass and blue-green mosses that filled the wedge-shaped areas between paths had suffered over the last weeks. Muddy spots marked where too many people had stood or walked, wearing down the greenery.

In contrast, the flowers at the center bloomed unabated. Long, curved blossoms of midnight blue touched with silver swayed atop tall blue stalks amid ample deep green foliage. Butterflies and songbirds danced above.

Nefeli's grandmother would have hated it, for she'd adored the sickly white stone Shadows. The country included many of them, all of which grandmother would regularly dance on whenever she passed by. Nefeli's mother had once joked that when the old woman wanted to invade a country she'd pick the nearest land possessing a Shadow, or a city-state between Codaros and the nearest Shadow.

Just a joke, but with enough truth in it to bite. Nefeli's mother had never voiced it anywhere the old woman could hear, or to anyone who might let it slip.

Her grandmother's hatred alone offered Nefeli reason enough to favor the change.

HER PLACE ON THE WIDE CIRCULAR STONE PATH OFFERED HER excellent views of the envoys as they left the woods and caught first sight of the flowers—though she missed the lead guards' reactions. They were spread out, ringing the clearing.

She'd spent most of the walk talking to the two envoys who'd first spoken the day before. They'd continued alternating comments, irritating but predictably so.

They froze. One gasped and clasped hands against their mouth. The other trembled for a moment. Then they jerked forward as though prodded from behind, and wound their way inward with hesitant steps.

Jola emerged next, smiling as she stepped aside. She took a deep breath, and a layer of stress seemed to melt off her.

Cahide stopped, mouth clearly agape under her veil. Her hands rose and she fiddled with the end of the fabric. Made it billow out, likely to bring in air that did not pass through the translucent fabric, but without actually removing it or allowing any of her face to be seen directly.

"Nightbells." Cahide sighed. "All thanks to the Lady Sun that I have lived to this day."

She practically floated across the expanse to hover near the blooms. The other envoys followed her, nearly as flower-beguiled as she, with Todor walking behind.

Jola paused near Nefeli. "Lady Sun?" she asked.

"I'm told the Erevestisi believe the sun watches over them," Nefeli said.

"Instead of our being of earth and to earth returning, as chance plays out?" Jola blinked, then shrugged.

"Indeed," Nefeli said. "But according to our librarians, we know less about this aspect of Erevestisi life than any other."

"Not that we know much in the first place." Jola ran a hand across Nefeli's back and smiled at her, then followed the Erevestisi to cluster near the nightbells.

Nefeli moved in as well, but remained far enough back to watch with ease the action around the blooms.

Most of the envoys remained there, but after a brief while two peeled away and approached her. One of the two envoys who'd walked with her—and who still had not shared a name—offered gratitude again.

"Our pleasure." Nefeli studied the figure, in particular the many-colored garments. A brief report from the librarians had suggested that the top layers indicated something of their wearers' interests. Cahide and the other two envoys still clustered in adoration wore shades of green, associated with sciences. The two who'd drifted closer to Nefeli had shades of blue predominant, which might denote trade.

So she delicately offered comments about Codaros's trading interests and the possibility of direct trade. The initial overtures were very well received, albeit couched in highly conditional language reserving all final decisions to the Council, of course, but Nefeli nevertheless enjoyed a strong feeling of satisfaction before a request to join the group by the bells.

No sooner than she had, then Cahide raised a question that drove all thought of trade away.

"Has anyone touched the nightbells?"

"Ah," Nefeli closed her mouth and glanced around in hopes of spotting a gardener who might answer.

"I understand that the gardeners tried to pick a bloom a few times, but couldn't." Rescue came from a most unexpected source. Todor stepped forward with a half-bow. "Other than that, most people don't come as close as you are now. They are content to admire from a distance."

"Indeed. But have any princesses or compeers attempted?"

"Not I, or anyone that I know of," Nefeli said.

"Nor me either. Princesses and compeers are mostly the same as others who visit, keeping a respectful distance." Jola tilted her head to the side. "Why do you ask? Do you know something we do not? The librarians have been searching for information about nightbells, but found little."

"It is not so much what I know, which is less than I like, so much as it is what I suspect," Cahide said.

Nefeli blinked, working through the implications. She caught Jola's glance her way, seeming to ask whether or not to continue, and nodded yes.

"Please," Jola said. "We would appreciate anything you are willing to share with us."

"Very well." Cahide took a step back and laid crossed hands over her chest. "Here are the fruits of my knowledge and my guessing, that they may benefit all of us. You must know that there are twelve or thirteen Shadows of the Moon, or there were before this changed." She waved at the swaying flowers. "Counts differ, nevertheless it is clear that the Shadows are spread about the continent roughly equidistant to each other."

"Equidistant?" Nefeli frowned. "Every map I've seen shows them scattered nearly at random."

"Equidistant in terms of travel. It is not that the Shadows are the same physical distance apart. One must take into account the nature of the terrain between them. Rather, it requires roughly the same amount of time to walk from any one to the next in a circuit. At least, twelve of them form a coherent travel trail around the land. The thirteenth, if it is a thirteenth, is different."

"Why does travel distance matter?" Jola asked.

"Because in the oldest tales, the stories of the first Dancing Princesses, they did not dance together save on very rare occasions. They could not. They did not live and work and dance together, as do you and your fellows. Instead, the accounts indicate princesses and compeers were scattered across the continent each in their own region with their own people until, all of a sudden, they vanished." Cahide lifted her hands from her chest and clapped once, then returned to her former pose. "There are gaps in the records, and few to no stories of princesses for generations. When once again princesses are mentioned, they live together in a group of twelve or thirteen in what has become Codaros."

"A natural change, perhaps." Nefeli hid her hands under the fall of her mantle, to conceal how her fingers twitched.

"Natural, maybe. Or not. The disappearance of the princesses has been a subject of interest in the halls at Erevestis for centuries. Of late we—I"—Cahide shrugged—"have wondered if the Shadows might mark where princesses were buried. News that this Shadow turned into flowers of myth, such as no one has seen for centuries, supports that theory but only if these are in truth nightbells. In which case, there is a means to test, for references in the oldest tales indicate nightbells sometimes speak with favored people and offer magical advice."

Flowers that spoke. Yet Nefeli could not laugh at the notion, not this close to the glorious blooms that had sprung up fully grown in the span of a night, or less.

Her gaze slipped to Jola, who'd made no mention of speaking blossoms when she shared her tale the night before. Surely she hadn't held that back?

Jola glanced Nefeli's way. She likely guessed at Nefeli's thoughts, for her lips tightened and she shook her head.

Then Todor stepped forward. "They do speak. Or, sort of."

"Truly?" Cahide trembled, hands clasped tight.

"What did they say?" Nefeli asked.

Todor met her gaze, then crossed his arms over his chest. "It was something small, meant for me."

His chin lifted, daring her to push. Which she would, but not here or in this company.

"If you do not mind, I would like to make an attempt," Cahide asked, dropping to her knees before Nefeli. "Perhaps you and Princess Jola would be willing to do so as well? And tell me if you hear anything? I do not ask for you to tell me *what* the flowers say if they speak to you, but knowing that they speak to more than one would be a boon."

An impossible request—refusal would offer insult, but how could Nefeli agree? The flowers would have to take care of themselves. They'd appeared so suddenly, Nefeli wouldn't be surprised if they had the ability to disappear equally fast. But speak to them herself, or ask Jola . . .

But the answer was taken out of her choosing.

$$\text{❧} \quad 2\,0 \quad \text{❧}$$

"I'll try." Jola stepped forward and offered Cahida a hand to help rise.

Memories of that strange night swamped Jola, overlapping with the current day. The strangeness, the bodies whisked from ground to by the wind and then carried away, and the flowers that manifested in their place. Something good had replaced evil, so surely if they did speak—of which Jola was not yet certain—they'd offer sound advice. Even if they did not, Jola did not have to heed it.

Nefeli jerked, reaching for Jola only to pull back. "I will as well, but as our guest would you care to go first?"

The twist in Nefeli's voice made clear she expected Cahide to agree, since the notion had come from her in the first place.

"Of course." Cahide laid her hand atop Jola's, though she didn't need the assistance to rise. The other envoys made weak protests, but Cahide paid no notice.

Though after she turned to face the flowers, she paused.

"Do you know how?" Todor asked.

"No. The stories didn't mention that." Cahide sighed.

"It's simple." He walked close and stretched out his arm so that his hand hovered over the flowers without touching them. The flowers stirred. Leaves rustled. Stalks straightened, so that the tips of the petals brushed Todor's palm. One after another, until all the flowers close enough had done so. A sigh seemed to ripple among the blooms too far away.

Pink tinged Todor's cheeks as he drew his hand back and cradled it against his chest.

He didn't say what the flowers shared.

Cahide tiptoed forward and mimicked his stance. Fewer blossoms reached for her, nevertheless at least five or six touched petal tips against flesh. She jerked, gasped, and slowly drew back.

Before Jola could do the same, Nefeli squeezed her shoulder. "Let me first, to make sure all's well."

The soft words held Jola in place as Nefeli held her hand as far as she could over the center of the flower bed.

Nearly all blooms reached for her, rustling and stretching. Petal after petal touched, not merely tips but midway down. The clearing was quiet enough for all to hear the catch in Nefeli's breath. She pulled back, eyes damp and wide and not focusing on anyone.

Jola drew in a deep breath, then took her turn. She followed Nefeli's example, stretching her hand in far, and was rewarded when as many flowers reached for her.

Softness.

Warmth.

Welcome.

The nightbells' perfume filled her, and the each succeeding wave of soft, warm, welcome seemed to wrap around her as though the blooms enfolded her.

There were no words exchanged, or needed, but she drew back with clear understanding that the flowers desired, or was it wished? hoped? expected? to see her Dance.

Soon.

The feel of the petals lingered. The slightest touch of anything soft or warm, no matter that it was inevitably rougher or cooler, brought the sensation back. Even hours later, back in her and Nefeli's rooms after dinner, all Jola had to do was close her eyes and she was cradled among the nightbells.

Jola reclined on her couch—velvety but nowhere near the petals—and wrapped her fingers around a mug of sweet water. Nefeli matched her on the other couch.

They'd both removed their formal embroidered mantles, which hung in their bedroom until they could be brushed and folded and put away. Jewelry from circlets to bracelets and anklets were piled on the table by their bed. Sandals sat abandoned by the door.

Yet neither had changed from their tunics, still gathered at the waist by cords of twined gold and silver. The loose skirts pooled around their legs, pink for Jola and soft green for Nefeli.

Jola half-dozed, listening to Nefeli but not absorbing every word. Nefeli ticked back and forth between puzzling over all that Cahide had shared about the Shadows, and the possibility of direct trade with Erevestis.

Yet nary a word about the flowers speaking. No questions about Jola's experience or what she'd heard. Nor any confidence as to what the blossoms had said to Nefeli.

Nothing. The few times Jola had tried to raise the topic, Nefeli had not seemed to realize.

But neither, despite the late hour, did she show any interest in heading to bed.

Until a knock on the door stopped Nefeli mid-word. Her eyes glinted as she rose to answer.

She must have expected it. Even arranged it. The table with the pitcher of sweet water held an extra mug, something Jola had noticed and ignored until too late.

Todor entered, nearly as casually dressed as Jola and Nefeli, except he still wore sandals and a sash belted his deep blue tunic. He nodded to Nefeli, then Jola, and declined to settle on the couch in Nefeli's place.

Nefeli remained standing, the two close in height and looks although they stood several feet apart.

After a moment, Jola rose rather than be the only one seated. She entwined her fingers and waited.

"You wanted to talk to me?" Todor asked Nefeli, glancing at Jola.

"Should I leave?" Jola started toward the bedroom and took all of two steps before Nefeli called her back.

"No, stay, darling. This may concern you."

Jola turned back around, only to watch the siblings stare at each other.

Nefeli spoke first. "I didn't ask earlier, but what did the flowers say to you?"

Stiff and arms tight against his side, Todor lifted his chin. "It's personal

"I'm not asking out of whim." Nefeli grabbed a handful of curls and yanked, then grimaced and pulled her hand back. "I need to know."

Todor lifted an eyebrow.

"Not everything, not anything truly private," Nefeli moved closer, until only a few breaths separated them. Energy poured off her in waves—energy, or worry? "Did they say anything of our grandmother?"

Todor jerked, stumbling backward until he pressed against the door.

Although Jola had never met the old Terparchon, she lurched in sympathy. By the time she'd been at court a year, she'd heard stories by the dozen about the unlamented ruler who brooked no opposition. The unflinching leader who demanded princesses and compeers Dance to the last gasp to protect things she valued above people. The land-hungry despot who nearly doubled the size of Codaros and was only prevented from adding on more territory by her daughter deposing her.

"Grandmother's dead. I saw the body. I *touched* her." Todor dug fingers into the door, lips drawn in a snarl. "I couldn't believe she was gone until that."

"I touched her corpse too." Nefeli pried Todor off the door, rubbing his shoulders as she ushered him over to sit on her couch. She settled next to him, face ashen. "But the flowers—"

"What about the flowers?" Todor asked.

Jola settled back on her couch. Grabbing the pitcher, she filled the extra mug and pressed it into Todor's hands. He drained it in a moment.

"They didn't speak in words, not to me, but there was a sense of my being a sibling of sorts. That they considered me mother's heir and wanted me to rule well," Nefeli paused, then swallowed hard and continued, "and keep the land from my grandmother's hands."

"They said nothing of grandmother to me. If they had, I don't know as I'd have told you about them talking." Todor held out the mug for a second round, which he drank equally fast. "But she's dead!"

"Maybe they don't want you to follow in her footsteps?" Jola asked.

"Maybe. That would be acceptable. Do-able." Nefeli wrinkled her nose. "She used to dance on the Shadow, every Shadow, at least once a year. But there's . . ." her voice trailed off. She rubbed her forehead.

If they were alone, Jola would have gone over to rub Nefeli's shoulders and back, and comfort her. Jola could have, if Nefeli had been willing to share the news with her alone, first, before bringing Todor into the mix. But at least she was included, though she had little to offer.

"The flowers didn't mention your grandmother to me, either. The only thing they shared with me was an expectation that I'd Dance for them sometime."

"We'll have to arrange that, then, before we leave." Nefeli managed a smile, then sneezed.

Todor coughed at the same moment.

Jola choked as a sudden stench of smoke turned the air pale gray. Bits of ash flickered into life around them only to blaze and vanish.

Dozens of bells—from high to low—set up a clamor. But these bells were felt, not heard, ringing in Jola's bones in a fury of anger . . .

And fear.

"What is that?" Todor leapt to his feet and pointed out the window, still coughing.

Hand clasped across her mouth and nose, Jola followed as did Nefeli. They pressed hard against the side of the window, barely able to see the sullen glow of flames in the distance.

"It's in the gardens, over near the Shadow."

"The nightbells." Jola's teeth ached, chattering as she forced the words out, sudden understanding flooding her. "They're burning!

Nefeli hated running at night, in the dark, through the woods. Finding her way wasn't a problem. The earth remembered where feet had passed, especially after so many palace denizens had visited the clearing and former Shadow since the change. Her feet pounded along the track with ease, even barefoot. The *rest* of her body suffered. Spiderwebs stretched across parts of the path at several points, particularly where the bushes on either side narrowed to allow only one person to pass at a time.

Birds hooted in the distance. Bats curvetted in small groups, fuddled by the haze of smoke that hung in the air, coating Nefeli's tongue and throat. One nearly flew right into her face before darting off as its wing tips brushed her cheek. Another went right into her tunic skirt, whipping around her legs, and flapped several times before ripping free. Nefeli hiked her skirt higher, tucking folds under her belt, just in time for another bat to dazedly dart between her legs.

Luminescent growths offered subtle light to either side, but increasingly frequent flashes of ruddy light ahead made it hard to adjust back and forth between less light and more.

Heated breath warmed the back of her neck whenever she slowed. Every footfall pinged her senses, reminding her over and over of who followed. Todor, Danissa, other princesses and compeers, guards, and a host of more boiling out of the palace with calls for the water brigade but the wagons were on the wrong side of the palace and too wide for any of the near paths.

Nefeli tried to draw her senses back. She didn't truly need them to find her way. Jola ran ahead. Her bright skirts flickered in the light—luminescent or ruddy—showing where to follow.

The path widened briefly. With a storm of footfalls and heavy breaths, two guards whipped past her and up before Jola. The bronze rank markings on their boots glimmered as they forged ahead, clearing the way.

Evidently they, too, guessed this couldn't be a natural fire. No storm, no flash of lightning anywhere. True, the strike that had reputedly changed the Shadow to nightbells in the first place had come in the middle of a calm night after a storm—but there were witnesses even in the palace who'd seen the flash and heard the thunderclap.

Nothing of that sort this night.

But who would hurt the nightbells and why?

More immediately, the problem of putting the fire out loomed. The lake was too far for a bucket brigade. The water wagons might make the long way around. One of the guards had a cloak, would it work to beat at flames?

The best way: Dance the fire down.

"We'll need all princesses and compeers." Jola turned her head for a moment, clearly thinking along the same lines.

Before Nefeli could respond, Todor, behind her, took up the call and passed it back.

Nefeli let her senses follow the line of folk behind her. Idan was there, and Leta. Ylena and Solon were missing, though Ylena might need to be carried.

Her eyes smarted as the smoke grew. The air turned hazy. Her throat tightened, lungs protesting the thickness. Guards and Jola ahead slowed, and so did Nefeli.

Her power stretched ahead, untrammeled by the smoke. The last twists of the path stood out plain in her mind's eye—and the clearing beyond.

And the sole person dancing a jagged, uneven circle around the center.

No, Dancing.

Solon.

Each footstep fell heavy on the earth as though he leapt high and thumped down with all his might. The earth beneath recoiled. Tiny tremors rippled through the dirt, for the impact hit with more than weight. Bitterness pressed down, seeped into the cracks.

No one else. Only his feet—and they were most definitely his. He'd been a princess long enough Nefeli couldn't mistake him for anyone else.

"It's Solon. He's the only one there." Burning out literally and taking the flowers with him? It made no sense, except his stomps reminded her of the horrid, ghastly Shadow that had once loomed in the clearing—with a hint of something else. Something more. Something familiar.

"Heard." Jola had no time to say anything more.

Nefeli had a moment's warning that the guards' feet stopped. Their abrupt stillness and press against the earth made her slow.

But Jola ran right into their backs. They grabbed for the trees to either side and pushed back, sending Jola reeling. Nefeli caught her, squeezing Jola's shoulders as she set her lover to rights. Further back, the trail of followers jerked and lurched as they also stopped.

Only with the thuds of footsteps ceasing did fire's crackle register.

Bright orange and red flames surged waist-high only a few feet ahead of the guards. They'd reached the edge of the clearing, but had little room to maneuver. Nefeli's rib muscles ached as she leaned to the side to peer around them.

A thin line of fire circled the clearing, stretching higher than wide but formidable for all that. Each flickering flame released a gout of grayness-smoke or ash or both. Nefeli pulled the neckline of her tunic up over her nose and mouth. Blinking helped only a little, as bits of ash clung to her lashes.

A second circle burned mid-way through the clearing, also waist-high.

The bonfire at the center dwarfed both. How could the flowers survive?

Yet Solon Danced on. His off-key voice occasionally rose above the crackling flames, breaking high as he chanted "burn it down, burn it down." His arms jerked as he turned around. Despite the distance, his face seemed a blank when he glanced their way. He wore a calf-length white tunic, the plain attire they usually Danced in. It shone against the poisonous green light that limned his body.

"This isn't burnout." Nefeli's hands chilled, despite still holding Jola's warm, sweaty body.

Jola didn't seem to hear. Braced against Nefeli, she was studying the fires. "The outer ring is the weakest."

The guards dug their heels into the earth, loosening dirt to throw on the flames. It was hard packed, resisting their efforts. One called back for buckets.

The movement opened space between them—narrow but just enough for someone determined to get through. Nefeli had no warning when Jola slipped from her grasp and leaped.

"Jola!" Nefeli shrieked, even as the guards and Todor and the others close enough to see cursed.

Nefeli watched, one hand pressed against her mouth. Her breath caught in her throat as her chosen princess used the small expanse of space perfectly to rise high.

Jola pulled her feet up, catching her legs close against her body as she cleared the tips of the flames by a finger's breadth, and landed gently on the other side.

"What are you doing?" Nefeli pushed the guards aside. One hit a tree and the other whirled behind.

Strangely, this close the fire gave off no heat. If anything, it carried a chill. Goosebumps lined Nefeli's legs as she drew near.

"Making room for us to Dance." Jola straightened. The flames lit her face from the bottom-up, painting her skin and gown in ruddy flickers. She stretched out a hand, fingers trembling.

Not a command or a plea.

But Nefeli couldn't, wouldn't, let Jola face this danger without her.

"Pull back." She turned to the guards and Todor. "Don't let anyone follow us, yet."

Without waiting to see they obeyed, or pausing long enough to think twice, she squatted down. The earth rocked beneath her, and as she leapt it pushed giving her additional momentum. She rose and tumbled forward with less grace than Jola, but greater height and distance.

Nefeli landed hard. Her feet struck the earth between the outer rings of flame, causing motes of deep, seething green to flicker around her feet and then subside. The bits that fell on her feet and ankles clung, making her skin itch.

The smoke lessened, but had a greenish tinge and tasted of pure bitterness. Impossible to dispel, no matter how often she swallowed.

"What now?" she asked.

"We have to dance the outer fire down, so the rest can get through." Jola waved at the crowded path behind—where numerous faces watched over the flames although no one yet dared follow. "And then deal with Solon and the bonfire."

"Or deal with Solon first." Nefeli shivered as Solon continued his jerky circle without seeming to notice Jola and Nefeli's drawing closer. The unusual heaviness of his footsteps increased, although he barely raised his feet above the earth.

"No," Jola said, chest heaving as she took a deep breath. "We'll need the others for that."

"But not the outer fire?"

"This is easier, I think." Jola's smile flashed and vanished. "We help the earth and air remember the last storm. Here's the beat."

Jola laid a warm hand against Nefeli's shoulder. Her fingers tapped thrice, paused, and repeated the quick step.

The next moment, Jola was off leaving a cool spot behind on Nefeli —nothing like the chill of the flames. Jola twirled and leapt, tossing her hands as though grabbing lightning and rain and casting them down. Her fingers flicked at the non-existent rain at the outer circle of flames.

After a moment's watching, Nefeli followed. Quick steps brought her to Jola's side at just the right moment to lift the princess high. Jola reached and flicked as Nefeli lowered her down.

Then Jola whirled around and repeated the movements in the opposite direction. Nefeli followed without missing a beat. No matter how Jola moved, how fast her leaps quickened as she followed the circle all the way around, Nefeli matched her. Time and again her hands grasped Jola's waist and lifted her.

Grace. Glory. Magic.

They were made for this, not just to Dance but to do so *together*. They kept the beat, blood pounding equally in two hearts, two bodies, joined by internal music and shared movement.

Sweat dripped down Nefeli's face. Her tunic plastered to her chest, back, and legs. Jola's likewise clung to the princess, from her own perspiration and the press of Nefeli's hands at her waist.

With every leap, every whirl, every flick of Jola's fingers, the smoke lessened. The air grew humid. Nefeli's nose twitched at the astringent scent that heralded coming rain.

A faint flicker of lightning streaked across the sky.

Not a single raincloud loomed, yet drops began to fall. Jola twirled and leaped as she finished the circuit, with Nefeli at her side.

The outer ring sputtered as rain spritzed into existence then cascaded exactly along the lines of fire. The flames guttered, dying slowly as Jola and Nefeli did a second round, this time Jola flicked rain at the middle ring.

They weren't alone. Todor and Danissa crossed the lowering outer ring and joined them.

Jola smiled and waved for them to follow behind—but it was Nefeli who ensured they maintained the right amount of space between them for maximum power.

More moisture filled the air. Lines of rain formed above the failing flames.

But the seething cold fire burned on.

Nefeli's body thrummed with the triple beat that Jola had set. Her hair slicked against her forehead, and she dashed a hand to keep it out of her eyes as she followed Jola.

Lift.

Flick.

Lower.

Repeat.

As they finished the second round, Ylena had reached the end of the path. Her crutches leaned against a tree as she sat on the other side of the flames. Her hands waved and bobbed, summoning water.

Two more joined in the dance—Idan and Leta stepping over the line of flames now dark orange against the shadowy earth. Both compeers, they wouldn't dance together.

Jola waved for them to split. Idan joined Todor and his daughter. Leta aligned herself with Nefeli.

"Lift and carry." Jola gasped, chest heaving.

Nefeli had already shifted into motion. One last time her hands wrapped around Jola's waist and raised her high. Then she slipped forward and Leta back, supporting Jola between them as they raised her above their heads.

A soft grunt from behind indicated Idan and Todor did likewise with Danissa.

One last round filled the air with moisture and turned the outer and middle rings to piles of ash smoldering against damp moss and grass.

The inner bonfire around the flowers remained.

Solon capered around, gaze vacant and making no sign that he'd noticed them though surely he had.

This close, without the distraction of the outer flames, The heavy thump of Solon's feet renewed the bitterness in Nefeli's mouth. The air gleamed ever greener around him, a poisonous shade she'd seen nowhere else.

Almost nowhere else.

For the earth under Solon's feet shivered and ached in a way Nefeli had felt only certain times before.

She swallowed, but a bitter lump remained in her throat as she panted. Alongside Leta, she lowered a dripping Jola to stand between them.

Sweaty she might be, but Jola started forward to storm ahead and confront Solon or so Nefeli guessed from the way her body lurched.

Nefeli matched her, this time slipping hands under Jola's arms to hold her back by the shoulders.

"Let go." Jola whirled, anger flaring in her eyes—a glitter only distantly kin to the light around Solon. "It takes a princess to face down another princess."

"It's not just Solon there. You need to know before you face him." Nefeli drew in a hissing breath, lungs aching. "He's not burning out, or not just burning out."

"Then what *is* going on?"

Nefeli shivered, although Todor, Danissa, and Idan had joined Leta in a semi-circle around her and Jola, warmth pouring off their bodies.

"Solon carries a taint on him." Nefeli glanced back and forth between Jola and Todor. Neither would be surprised, surely, and yet perhaps . . . "Somehow this is the work of my grandmother."

❧ 2 2 ☙

Jola crossed her hands over her chest, pressing palms against shoulders as she drew in deep, ragged breaths. Sweat covered her, head to toe, but the night air already started wicking away the moisture and leaving chill behind. Her tunic clung to her skin, hair slicked against her head save where the bulk remained pinned close, and the others weren't much better off.

A bitterness hung in the air, impossible to be rid of no matter how often she swallowed. Not smoke, not fire, but rather as though she'd eaten something overripe. Whispers floated over from the path, where dozens of eyes peered and gleamed in the flickering light of the bonfire.

Jola planted her feet wide, toes digging into the moss as she remained upright. The fire burned atop the nightbells to her right. Ash coated the flowers, turning them gray tinged with unhealthy green. Even glancing out of the corner of her eyes made them water, as Solon tramped around. He hardly made any movements with hands, arms, head, or hips—yet his feet sent solid thuds as he turned around and around. A green miasma hugged his body, glowing and betraying his every movement even to her blurry sight.

Worse, power seethed beneath him. The flames might whisk along the long petals as they turned to ash, but a second set flickered in the earth below. Lapped at the flowers' roots. Crackled louder with Solon's every circuit.

Otherwise, silence settled over the small group of princesses and compeers.

Only then did Nefeli's words register.

"Your grandmother."

Perhaps Jola should have expected something of the sort. How long since Nefeli had asked Todor about references to Nefeli's grandmother in the nightbell's whispered messages? Less than an hour at most.

Of all present, only Nefeli, Todor, and Idan had Danced for the old Terparchon. Todor flinched, arms pressing inward. Idan startled, then nodded.

"It has her touch."

Yet in Jola's surprise, she noted that Nefeli seemed grim as though this were no more than she'd expected. Even if she'd had suspicions since speaking with the nightbells, this seemed odd.

Or had she had glimmerings earlier?

But this was no time for Jola to ponder the matter. At best, half the fire had faded. The worst lay before them.

Jola turned a full circuit, taking in everything and everyone she could. Who was there and in what condition. Todor, Danissa, Idan, and Leta close and warm from their earlier exertions but still with energy, Nefeli likewise. Ylena's form unmistakable over by the edge of the clearing, also possessed of a store of energy.

Guards and courtiers and servants lining the paths off into the distance, perhaps Cahide and some of the other Erevestisi envoys mixed among them but for the most part they were blurs of shadow and darkness. The distant creak of the water wagon, but it wouldn't arrive in time.

Bracing against the bright green-tinged orange of the flame, Jola faced Solon.

His face was a blank, empty of emotion and thought. His body jerked, the miasma seething along his skin.

No, Nefeli had it right earlier. This wasn't burnout for him, or time for Jola to worry about herself. The flowers, the miracle that had replaced the horror of the Shadow, had wanted to see Jola Dance.

They'd get their wish.

Solon was one princess.

Jola had two others on her side, and four compeers. Hardly a full thirteen plus thirteen, but they'd make do.

Fear snaked up her spine. Might she wind up taken over and Dancing as blankly as Solon?

No. Jola refused. No time for fears or worries. If she burned out, she'd face life after. Considering how many burned-out princesses and compeers ran the dance exchange programs in the land's many cities, life would continue regardless.

A rill of energy ran along the bottom of Jola's feet, followed by another and another. Then a pause, after which the triple rills repeated.

Jola bent and laid a hand against the earth. The same beat pressed against her palm.

An order? Request? Incipient burnout?

Rising, she turned to face the paths. She clapped her hands to match the beat. "Keep this." Two more sets of three beats followed by a pause, and the sound echoed from every corner of the clearing.

Everyone picked it up, even the Erevestisi.

The ground resounded with it.

"Idan, Leta," Jola whirled, pointing at them. "Bring Ylena out to Dance. Carry her as needed. Be earth and stone. Focus on resisting flame and corruption. Fire may scorch, but will never reduce you to ash."

They nodded and whirled off to fetch Ylena.

"Danissa, Todor, be moisture and air. Bring rain, as before, and enough to dampen the flowers from petals to roots." Danissa rose on tip toe, then darted in dainty steps starting a wide zigzag circle. Todor followed, mimicking her gestures.

"What will we dance?" Nefeli matched Jola's posture, a warm line along her side.

"Resistance." Jola bent. Pulled arms and torso down toward her legs, then drew herself up to her full height. Arms loose at her side and body limber, she copied Solon's movements but moved in reverse.

Almost reverse, for where he thudded she tiptoed, with Nefeli right behind.

His face remained blank, mumbling about burning things down. Jola smiled and laughed as she imagined the flowers watching beneath their coating of ash, as Nefeli lifted and twirled her around.

The shrinking coat of ash.

The flames stuttered, but remained. A haze of rain manifested, and dampness crept along the plants' roots. The other princesses and compeers fluttered in and out of Jola's vision, but she didn't need to see to know where they were. Magic filled the air with the perfume of the nightbells mixed with human sweat.

But the bitter, poisonous tang remained.

Jola Danced light and lightness, but aches spread along her muscles and her bones seemed heavy.

Her arms started to hang loose at her side, too accurate a mimicry of Solon's stumbled movements.

She couldn't let her Dance be solely the opposite. Resistance wasn't enough. Each princess Danced separately. Ylena, Danissa, Jola, each effective but no match for Solon's unblinking focus.

With a start, Jola dropped onto her heels. She swayed, body stiff, and nearly fell.

Nefeli caught her. A familiar arm wrapped around Jola's waist. Beautiful brown eyes gazed into Jola's, full of confidence and faith in her.

Jola ran a hand along Nefeli's cheek, and let that be the first move of a different Dance. Not resistance but persistence. Continuity in the face of grief, danger, and destruction.

Instead of copying and twisting Solon, Jola returned to her earlier movements. No matter the aches along her legs, she leapt and twirled. With each whirl, she gathered the power Ylena and Danissa raised, shaped with their compeers' assistance.

More energy poured in from the watchers, the clappers providing the music and hearts full of hope and good will.

Jola even whisked up a trace of power from Solon, finding his will at war within himself.

With every step, Nefeli matched Jola. Balanced her when she nearly tipped over. Guided her away from the occasional stone buried within the moss. Helped her bring together the disparate sources of power and direct it into the flowers.

Rejection of the heat, the flames, the fire and ash.

Denial of the miasma.

Strength and fortitude.

The flowers shivered. The cloud of ash and flames burst. Motes flickering into embers flew high in the air, where a sudden burst of wind carried them off.

Solon jerked and collapsed into a heap. The poisonous green light lifted from his body. For a moment it seethed as though form and substance—but with a twirl, Jola summoned more wind to carry it off.

The flowers burst into exuberant bloom, singed but emitting an even more intense perfume that lifted the spirit.

Jola settled onto the earth, bending and heaving as she dragged in uneven breaths. Nefeli was in a similar state, though she kept one warm hand braced against the center of Jola's back.

The clapped beat turned into cheers. The moss beneath Jola's feet gave a last triple beat then drummed for several breaths before subsiding into usual quiet.

Catching her breath, Jola straightened and waved for guards to come take Solon to the infirmary.

"Are you sure?" Todor panted nearby, Danissa a heap on the earth beyond him with her father at her side.

"No, it's the right thing. It wasn't just him." Nefeli held Jola, supporting her body and orders. "Grandmother got to him somehow, no matter how long she's been dead. But she over did it. Solon is no longer a princess."

Todor drew in a hissing breath.

"Burned out?" Danissa asked.

"No. He's no longer a princess in any way shape or form, as though he never Danced a step." Nefeli turned and buried her face against

Jola's shoulder for a long moment. Then she lifted her head and scanned Jola, perhaps for signs of injury or exhaustion. "How are you?"

"Still a princess." Magic thrummed in every bone and muscle in Jola's body. She no longer feared burning out any time soon. Surety filled her that instead she'd found a deeper understanding of Dance, a gift once or forevermore for weaving disparate dancers into a whole. "And strong enough to match you in the Dance whenever and however you need."

Jola's pleasure in her new connection to dance magic doubled at the joy in Nefeli's eyes as she understood: Jola was as suitable to be the next Terparchon as Nefeli the next Marchon.

Only a faint worry or two lingered.

Nefeli hadn't mentioned her grandmother for a long time. Nor had she let slip any hint of a secret even as she'd unraveled the tangled strands of Jola's.

Just when had Jola's lover realized some wisp of her grandmother's bitterness remained?

ef{#}   2 3   ef{#}

Nefeli's leg twitched. Few seemed notice, despite the bright light baskets turning the hastily opened reception room almost as bright as day. Her foot tapping made soft sounds, sandal pressing against soft woven rug and thus lost amid the general flurry of questions, comments, and answers. Too much of the first, too little of the last. Perhaps the folds of the clean, plain tunic she'd donned after a quick pass through the bathing rooms hid the movement, but surely people had to head back to bed soon?

Jola, at least, was aware. She shared the couch with Nefeli, although she reclined against the far end rather than sitting straight with feet on the floor. Impossible for her to miss, surely the twitching reverberated through the cushions. Yet she leaned against the sofa arm, quietly watching the the others speaking in turn.

All the dancers were present, all seven princesses and compeers with only Solon off in the infirmary. Even Ylena sat on a couch across the way, her crutches on the floor beneath, and with a smile because the healers had agreed she could go to her own chambers after the discussion rather than heft back across the breadth of the palace complex. Idan occupied a couch as well, after his daughter made clear he shouldn't be pacing since he, too, was still healing. Instead Danissa paced, occasionally pausing in the far corner where her new lover, a librarian, had managed to sneak in and stay.

Todor also remained on his feet, moving restlessly from window to window, couch to couch, without pausing long enough even to take advantage of the spiced water and hastily prepared fruits laid out on a side table. Leta stood at a window offering a view across the complex at the infirmary, her face a study in puzzlement.

Nefeli could order them all off to bed, but that would upset long-standing practice that any *new* Dance be discussed immediately after to fix memories of what worked and what didn't.

If only she shared Jola's ease and serenity—though that had to be partly a mask. For Jola insisted they gather to discuss the Dance. Jola who'd ensured the servants opened the room and provided food and drink. Jola who allowed the librarian to attend when Danissa asked.

At least Jola hadn't agreed to include Cahide, who'd clearly wanted to listen in. The Erevestisi had accepted encouragement to return to her chambers with diplomatic politeness.

And a soft-voiced aside to Nefeli that, if Nefeli would be so kind, Cahide would appreciate accompanying the court to the winter palace to pay her respects to the Terparchon in person.

But that could wait for daylight, or another day or three, to decide.

Nefeli's other leg began twitching as well, setting up a soft, tandem drumming.

Jola leaned over and laid a hand on Nefeli's shoulder. Nefeli stopped moving, all sensation centered on that single point of warmth connecting them. Their gazes met. Nefeli found caution and puzzle-ment on Jola's face, but couldn't be sure what showed on hers.

Jola brushed Nefeli's cheek in a brief caress, then rose and clapped her hands. It was everyone else's turn to still. A thrill of pride rippled through Nefeli as her lover took the role of the Terparchon in post-Dance reviews.

"Let us put together a summation of what happened, as clear as we can be while we still remember." Jola nodded at the librarian, poised with a stylus and board. "Details may be added later, for it is late and we all can use sleep."

She glanced around, meeting everyone's gaze one at a time. This was the princess Nefeli had always known Jola could be, certain of her strength and value. She'd shuffled off fears of burnout, secure in the unusual Dance she'd designed and managed with no time to prepare.

"Solon cannot add to our knowledge at this time. He is under the care of the healers, and no longer a princess, but I am sure he will offer what he can later." Jola settled back onto the couch, cushions creaking as she tucked her feet under. "This is what we know without him. First, that he was suffering from burnout, though fighting it. Second, that he seems to have somehow come under the influence of the former Terparchon. Perhaps the burnout made him vulnerable, but that is speculation. We may never learn the full tale. Regardless, the result was a determination to destroy the flowers. Why? Again, unknown."

"The old Terparchon loved the Shadows of the Moon." Idan's voice was hoarse, and he coughed. His daughter flew to kneel at his side with a goblet of spiced water and coaxed him to drink before continuing. "She used to dance on them, and would've hated the destruction of this one, and hated the flowers."

"This is good to know, but still speculative. Under this influence, or of his own volition, Solon tried to destroy the nightbells. He laid multiple magical fires, and Danced such malice . . ." Jola shivered. "I wouldn't have guessed him capable of it, but it took all of us to Dance the earth to reject the fire and preserve the flowers."

"I think he might've tried to turn the flowers back into the Shadow." Danissa held tight to the arm of her father's couch, still kneeling by his side.

Her comment unleashed a floodgate of speculation and suggestions. This, that, the other. Arguments over how burnout manifested, whether it made people more vulnerable to suggestions, whether turning the flowers back to the Shadow could work. So many things.

Yet so much delicate tiptoeing around the matter of the old Terparchon.

Nefeli's legs started twitching again. She'd barely wet her lips on water, and eaten nothing, still her stomach seemed heavy within her.

After a bout of coughing that quieted most discussion, Idan asked

Jola how certain she was that Solon was overlaid with some residue of the old Terparchon.

Jola hesitated, glancing at Nefeli out of the corner of her eye. The look hit Nefeli as hard as if she'd been slapped.

Todor spoke up first, when it became clear Jola would not. "We were just talking about grandmother," he waved at Jola and Nefeli, head tilting to the side.

It was a pointed kindness, from someone known more for the latter than the former. He hadn't shared Nefeli's message from the flowers, or so much as hinted at it, but made clear he was deferring to *her* and expected her to provide some measure of information.

Nefeli stiffened in surprise, noting raised eyebrows from Jola and Ylena as well. The weight in her belly eased slightly. She nodded at him, giving permission to share in her place to see what he'd do—the brother who should be a princess but, thanks to their grandmother's constant whittling down, had never developed more than a hint of princess magic.

"The nightbells gave Nefeli a message earlier," Todor said. "To keep the land from our grandmother's hands."

Quiet. Stillness.

Shock, clear on the faces of those who'd had the most to do with the old Terparchon, who'd Danced under her—Idan, Leta—or close to those who had—Danissa.

Unease showing on the rest, who'd at most brushed the fringes of the court before Nefeli and Todor's mother took over: Ylena, Jola, and the librarian in the corner.

"I don't like this." Of all of them, Idan had known the former Terparchon the longest. "Not one big. Death is death until rebirth, and this is not rebirth." He shuddered. "But perhaps this will be the only time?"

No certainty in his voice.

The weight in Nefeli's belly increased. Pressing hands against her midsection, she rose.

"I fear it won't be." She said.

More quiet, to the point that the cry of a stray bird out over the lake nearly echoed in the stillness. The same reactions as before showed on her listeners, but deeper. Heavier. Muscles tensed.

Jola watched, a deep line furrowing her brow.

She dared break the silence first, standing opposite Nefeli. "Why?"

"I'm sorry. I wish I never had to share this. Or that there were a better time." Nefeli met Jola's gaze. Tried to convey she'd prefer to speak with Jola first, but the rest deserved to know as well. "I felt my grandmother's footfall one other time this summer."

Tearing away, turning away from Jola, Nefeli stared at Idan—the only other born compeer present who might have felt the same. "Did you?"

Idan, too, rose, back straight and shoulders unbowed but hands flexing rhythmically at his sides. "When?"

"During the solstice dance." Nefeli said.

Idan flinched, arms drawing tight against his body.

"It was just a flicker," Nefeli continued. "A moment before Ylena tripped, and right next to her."

"You're saying *she* tripped me?" Ylena leaned forward, fingers curved into claws. "The old Terparchon . . . but Solon wasn't anywhere near where I was dancing."

Idan dropped back into his seat, head in his hands. Jola whisked over to lay a comforting hand on Ylena's shoulder. Todor huddled back against the wall.

Nefeli remained in place, one moment watching Jola for signs of understanding of why she'd kept this secret, the next facing Ylena straight on. "I don't know if it was her doing. It was only a flicker, and only one moment. There and then gone, and then you were down. I believed I imagined it. Wanted to believe I had."

The quiet broke under the weight of a thousand questions, none of which Nefeli could answer. They bounced around her head, echoing the worries and but-she-couldn't thoughts she'd worn through ever since the moment. Her pulse pounded at her temples.

"Enough." Jola left Ylena's side and raised her hands. "You may discuss this more over the next days, but only among us" she waved at those in the room "until we can report to the Terparchon. For now, rest. The flowers survive, and we are all well, and that is as good an ending as we could ask for."

As a sign this was done, she headed toward the door—but stretched out a hand to Nefeli.

An order or an invitation? Certainly a suggestion to let the others go and rest, since the unwritten rules of the court insisted no one leave before the leaders.

Nefeli took Jola's hand and followed her down the hall and up stairs to their rooms. Despite the ache in her head, she was ready to face Jola's questions—and disappointment or whatever she might feel at Nefeli having kept the secret after pushing Jola to share hers.

But Jola instead encouraged Nefeli to lie down in bed. Brought cool, damp cloths to lay over both their foreheads, and cuddled behind Nefeli whispering they could speak the next morning.

They only delayed things. But she took the gentleness, and managed at length to fall asleep in the curve of her lover's body.

24

Jola woke to warmth. A woolen blanket covered her, blue and yellow stripes bright in morning light streaming through the window along with a draft carrying the scent of fruit pastries baking or cooling. Better still, Nefeli lay against Jola, side to side. Her lover slept on, breath whistling softly as she exhaled.

Slipping from the bed, Jola doubled the blanket over Nefeli, who turned but didn't wake. Jola's muscles ached, particularly along her arms and legs. She padded over to the toilet chamber, stretching as she went and wincing as sinews crackled and popped. The small room had a passthrough from the outer hall where a servant had left two pitchers. The smaller held plain drinking water, lukewarm to the touch. The larger still gave off a whiff of steam along with medicinal herbs. Jola soaked a clean cloth and pressed it against painful spots until the ache eased to a more managable level.

A thin, plain tunic offered warmth and little weight as she dressed, corralling the folds around her waist with a length of gilt-and-silver rope. Her hair she combed out, but left loose the better to warm her neck. So attired, she returned to the bedchamber and went to the window.

How many times over the past days, weeks, had she gazed off

trying to angle so as to see the clearing? Too many. She still couldn't spot it, only a wide green blur. No taint of smoke or ash tinged the air, and that was something.

Indeed, despite the herbed water a hint of the flowers perfume floated on the breeze.

Jola had Danced magic for nearly a decade, but always in underground chambers in the summer or winter palaces, or more rarely deep in the hearts of the realm's other major cities. Not until this summer had she seen, much less participated, in a Dance above ground. The very air seemed crisper, clearer, in the aftermath.

But not so strange that she missed the rustle of bedclothes and sense of being watched.

Nefeli had rolled over in bed and propped her head on a hand. "Good morning."

All ease and loose limbs, showing little sign of aches save a brief wince when stretching a calf, Nefeli came over to brush a wake-up kiss across Jola's lips.

An invitation to distraction, but Jola's stomach rumbled at the wrong time.

Or was it the right time, for that same crisp, clear air brought whispered memories of words spoken in the past—and secrets not shared until late.

"Ready for breakfast?" Nefeli clearly also felt the strangeness between them

"Certainly" Jola slipped from her lover's embrace to summon the meal. "After last night's Dance, we both need to eat well for health."

Breakfast of pastries and sliced fruit arrived with a tall stack of papers for Nefeli and a slightly smaller one for Jola. Most were open or folded and sealed, and a few decoratively arranged into fanciful shapes. A sign of the changes underway. Rustles and chimes underscored their meal as they reclined on their couches and dug into food and papers.

Jola's messages came primarily from princesses and compeers, or those caring for them. A report from the infirmary indicated Solon was downcast but physically recovering. Dorcia and Felix in the city offered assistance as needed. They'd felt a shift in the air overnight, and included subtle congratulations on Jola's anticipated promotion paired with a request for additional support for the dance program.

She shared the first with Nefeli, but not the latter.

Nefeli mostly grunted or sighed as she plowed through her pile along with her food.

So easy to imagine the two of them repeating this morning after morning—the meal, the paper, and the quiet with each lost in their own pile and little communication between them.

Most meals at court were formal to one degree or another. Always, they served multiple purposes and often feeding ranked as the least. Only the first meal of the day offered the possibility of the two of them together, doing whatever they chose without being watched or overheard.

But only if they chose to make it so. Nefeli hadn't spoken up. If Jola wanted exchange, she'd have to ask. Which she hadn't, much, over the years. Too shy at first, still astonished at the fortune that made Nefeli interested in *her*.

That persisted, even as Jola grew more comfortable in their pairing.

She'd have to change. Her breathing shallowed, teeth pressing into her lower lip. Scared still, to push for more, though Nefeli had offered proof after proof of her devotion.

Albeit without completely sharing.

Perhaps Nefeli wanted, needed, to be asked.

Drawing in a deep breath, Jola leaned forward to snag a pastry she wouldn't be able to eat, not with her stomach in knots, and waved at the piles next to Nefeli. "Anything of importance?"

Nefeli lifted her head and blinked at Jola, then shrugged. "Mostly small things, Logistical issues for hosting the envoys and our journey later. Cahide putting in an official request to accompany us north, you know the kind of thing."

With a rustle and grunt, Nefeli dropped a parchment creased from having been folded into the shape of a flower and picked up an open, flat expanse. She turned to it, away from Jola.

"Anything of interest?" A lump formed at the back of Jola's throat despite hard swallows.

"What?" Nefeli frowned, but at least turned her attention back to Jola.

Lump still in her throat, Jola licked her lips and let fall the first thing that came to mind. "Is this what your parents do?"

"I don't understand." Nefeli set the paper back down.

"Do they separately go through whatever papers await them in the morning?" Jola asked.

"I . . . don't think they eat breakfast together." Nefeli swung her legs over and sat facing Jola rather than at angles. Her mouth quirked to the side, sadness in her eyes. "I'm not sure they even sleep in the same bed. Or room."

"Is that what you want for us?"

Nefeli paused, considering the matter. Her brow furled and she said "no," then shrugged and waved at the papers. "I don't see what this has to do with my parents."

Setting her own papers aside, Jola got up and walked around the room, the better to breathe deeply and ease the tension growing in her shoulders. Easier to think, to come up with words when moving—whether they were good words or bad. She'd have to trust Nefeli to understand if they weren't right.

"When I grew up, there was always one meal—usually dinner—when we all sat down and talked about our days," Jola said. "My mothers would start, each sharing something, then the rest of us. And I know, because I listened at the door more than once, that later in the evening my mothers talked more, seeing how each was doing, and what they needed. I don't think we do enough of that."

"Talking in the evening?" Nefeli stood, but remained beside her couch.

"Talking at all."

"We are now."

"Yes, because I asked," Jola stopped pacing, extending a hand to show how it trembled. "It's not easy to ask. I don't want to presume, to push, to demand too much, so usually I wait. I waited for years for you to say you loved me."

"I thought I showed you, day in, day out." Nefeli wrapped Jola's shaking fingers in her warm hands.

"You did, but I needed the words to believe it would last. You gave them, at last, and that's what makes me bold to speak now."

Nefeli let go of Jola's hands and wrapped her in a warm embrace, repeating the words over and over. So many times that they filled Jola's head and she knew they'd echo back at her whenever she needed them to in the future.

⁜

NEFELI HELD JOLA CLOSE. ONE ARM WRAPPED AROUND HER LOVER'S waist. The other cupped Jola's face, as Nefeli brushed away tears with kisses and soft caresses. Her body heated where they pressed together, but a chill ran along her spine.

How had they got to this point? Nefeli's fault. She'd been so worried about secrets, her grandmother, becoming her mother's heir, that she'd barely spoken. Yet those were all recent distractions. She couldn't put the blame on them for not knowing, for having missed so long that Jola needed something Nefeli wasn't providing.

"I didn't know. I'm sorry, my love." She'd give Jola the words a thousand times a day if it would help. And help it was, as tension drained from Jola leaving her body loose and supple in Nefeli's embrace. More, Jola repeated the sentiments back almost as many times.

Nefeli had listened to Ylena accusing her of pulling Jola along—but only because it resonated with what Nefeli had always feared: that she, who had more power and place, was making all the decisions. She'd held back, for years, when she should have laid it all out.

Even if it meant Jola said no and turned away.

Better that than to leave Jola wondering.

"So sorry." Nefeli buried her face in Jola's loose locks.

"I understand," Jola shifted, pulling back far enough that Nefeli had to meet her gaze. "But sorry is only the beginning."

"Beginning of what?" Nefeli asked.

"Begin anew as we mean to go on." Jola bit her lip then straightened. "Which means we talk. We find time everyday, steal it if we have to, to make sure you know what I'm doing, and I know what you're facing."

"That sounds lovely." Nefeli freed one hand to rub her temple. Much as she wanted to promise the world, practical considerations crowded in right after. "But what if there is an emergency? Do we put ourselves first, over the country?"

"We find some way to balance what we need with what ruling demands, even if we have to fight for it. There has to be a way." Jola cupped Nefeli's face. "But I need you to tell me things: how you're feeling, what or who irritates you, what you're worried about."

Nefeli shivered. It meant making major changes, because Jola surely wouldn't be satisfied with just the who, where, and when. She's asked for more, the kinds of things Nefeli had kept to herself for so long. To ensure her grandmother didn't know, first. Then not hurt her mother or father when they couldn't help. And to protect her siblings from her grandmother.

Why else had Nefeli kept secret the flicker of her grandmother's presence she'd felt when Ylena tripped? Oh, she'd thought it was because she didn't believe it to be real, but then why hadn't she made it a joke, or at least told Jola?

If she'd shared more, would Jola have felt comfortable to return the favor with her own secrets?

Flutters in Jola's body, pressed against Nefeli's, suggested a return of tension as Jola waited for response.

"I'll try." Nefeli shook her head, standing straighter. That wasn't enough. "It will be a big change. I don't think you know how big a one."

"Tell me." Jola lifted her chin high, flickers of tension showing in the chill of her hands.

"I will, but also," Nefeli pulled back and wrapped Jola's hands in hers again. "Please, ask. Don't ever be afraid to ask. I may be angry at first, but at myself for not offering, for making you ask, until I can learn to offer first."

Jola swallowed, throat moving, but nodded.

Clearly, asking was as tough for her as offering would be for Nefeli. What a pair—but they could change. Nefeli would do it, to live up to Jola's hopes—and her own.

A bell rang in the distance, marking the passage of time and pressure of the world outside their rooms that would soon require them to leave.

"So," Nefeli gulped down a lump. "How do you want to go about this?"

"Let's begin as we want to go on." Jola led Nefeli back to their couches, but this time settled next to Nefeli. Their bodies aligned, offering warmth and comfort even as they faced the low table with the piles of papers. "Here's what's important that people sent to me."

Their heads bent together over the papers, offering a glimpse of their future doing this day after day.

Nefeli twined her fingers with Jola's as they moved from Jola's pile to Nefeli's and learned what they'd face in the days, weeks, years ahead.

Together.

25

Three months later, Nefeli strode down the wide hall at the center of the winter palace. The thick rug muffled her steps, colors still brightly gold and blue despite the number of people who passed over it any given day. Her sandal ties wrapped from ankle to knee, ensuring that her gold knit socks remained in place, though her toes were cold all the same. She hadn't fully adjusted to the approach of winter despite arriving in the north early in autumn. Her winter mantle was twice as long and three times thick as her summer, but she wore three layers of tunics beneath all the same, all in shades of red, and wrapped a long shawl around her head and neck.

Tapestries hung on the plastered walls between narrow marble columns. Half portrayed scenes from the lives of early Terparchons, mostly the same scenes as at the summer palace albeit very different in detail—Nefeli's ancestors had enjoyed glorifying themselves, and lacked a degree of imagination. The remaining tapestries showed glimpses of the countryside and cities. Bronze and glass lanterns affixed to the columns provided light, which reflected off the helmets and armor of the guards stationed at intervals. The Marchon had once joked that the guards were there to provide additional light as much or more than for protection.

The hall smelled of smoke even though only a single fire burned at the far end of the hall, in one of the closed stoves her father had convinced her mother to begin installing after taking over as Terparchon. It gave off more heat the closer she drew, but not enough to prevent the occasional draft.

Earlier when she'd gone out-of-doors to witness the Marchon's triumphal entry into the city, the air had the smell of snow, harbinger of a hard winter. Hardly a thought to make her happy.

But her father was back, at least, cheered into the city by a tolerant populace. She'd offered the official greeting, and received a kiss of peace, and the two sections of court had joined for a luxurious banquet before the new arrivals mostly hared off early to go to bed and rest after their long travels..

One day later, Nefeli headed for the large apartment her father shared with her mother, or supposedly shared, for a more personal welcome—and she did not plan to meet with him alone.

The rug swallowed the sounds of Jola's approach as much as it had Nefeli's footsteps, but Nefeli turned in time to smile and stretch out a hand. Jola wore even more layers than Nefeli, with four contrasting tunics and two mantles, both thinner than Nefeli's, and all of course in a mishmash of colors that made her something of a walking rainbow— albeit nowhere near so organized.

Still, Jola enjoyed the colors and that was what mattered. Some of the courtiers had begun to venture into more creative combinations as well, their imitation proving Jola's rising importance at court.

What pleased Nefeli more was the growing strength of their relationship. After taking time every morning to talk for a month, Jola had given Nefeli permission to locate her, even track her, as needed. She trusted Nefeli not to abuse the privilege. Nefeli hadn't, but not having to restrain her gift from reflexively reaching for Jola had unknotted something deep inside. Eased a tension Nefeli had barely realized existed until it dissipated.

"Are you ready?" Nefeli pulled Jola close enough to kiss her cheek.

"You're certain you want me with you for this?" Jola waved at the wide double doors, the wood lavishly decorated with immense bronze hinges, knobs, and locks. "The Marchon only arrived yesterday, and you've not met with him alone yet."

"We'll meet alone in time, when we want to get away and just be father and daughter." Nefeli squeezed Jola's hand. "But for this first meeting to discuss what's gone on since we parted, I would like you with me as my lover, my beloved, and my partner."

"In all things." Jola returned the caress, lifting her chin and squaring her shoulders.

"Whether or not he expects you." Nefeli finished.

"That's the part that may require explanation." Jola drew in a hissed breath.

Nefeli faced her square. "My mother once told me that as heir I would need to learn to presume to bring others with me on occasion. I'm practicing following her advice."

She'd left Jola behind before, and it had complicated things. Best to bring Jola with her now, so long as Nefeli's lover agreed, and show a united front.

Her magic flared, alerting her to movement on the other side of the door. The Marchon trod an oval circle in the wide room, around and around. He knew Nefeli was coming to see him.

With a smile at Jola and a last squeeze of her hand, Nefeli rapped on the door.

A moment later the right side opened. The Marchon himself stood there. He'd shifted to winter clothes, matching Jola for number of layers. And was that a second set of socks under his sandal ties? More notable than his clothes, however, were the lines on his face and the air of tiredness that hung about him. Even his broad smile of welcome didn't fully dispel that.

He glanced back and forth between them, then pulled the door wide to let them in. "Come and tell me all that I've missed. Dry words on paper are no replacement for truth shared face-to-face."

Rather than letting them rattle around the immense receiving room, he led them through an interior hall to a small chamber, plainly furnished. The tapestries on the wall showed mountain views, to match the prospect through the single window, which faced north and offered a vista of snow-capped peaks. The thick green rug showed divots where an immense chair usually sat in the center, perfect for gazing out the window, but it had been moved to the side. Another two chairs faced it, all of good solid wood and provided with ample cushions.

Evidently he'd guessed Nefeli might bring Jola with her.

He made no objection when Nefeli waved for Jola to take one of the two next to each other, and sat in the other herself.

The better to watch him as he listened, and to show that she and Jola were a matched pair.

The room lacked a stove or fireplace, but the stone wall beneath one of the tapestries must have had a source of heat on the other side, for it radiated warmth.

As did her father's smile at Nefeli, even though he did not make clear yet if he approved or not.

He listened and asked questions of both of them as they shared the details of the attack on the flowers and the rescue. The general outlines Nefeli had sent on ahead, but there was only so much one could write. Though she'd assured him and her mother that the flowers still bloomed well, if slightly scorched, when Nefeli and Jola had departed. Likewise she'd offered news of a possible trade agreement with the Erevestisi.

And that Cahide had come north to the winter palace.

"You've been busy," the Marchon said at the end.

"It wasn't our choice." Nefeli winced.

"It never is." He drew in a breath, then rose and walked the few steps across the room.

Nefeli and Jola both bolted to their feet rather than let him loom over them,

He laid a hand on Nefeli's shoulder and another on Jola's. "You've done well. I approve. Your mother will make the final call." He glanced between them, a hint of wistfulness in his gaze. "But if she asks my opinion, I will speak in your favor."

The wistfulness remained, mixed with tenderness, when he watched them leave his chambers an hour later.

They headed down and across the hall to their shared rooms. No more would Jola keep separate rooms elsewhere. Nefeli had asked her to move into her rooms, or choose a new suite to share, although they had yet to make a final decision.

"Well, that's done." Nefeli grabbed Jola and swung her around as soon as the door closed behind them, "Only mother's official approval to go."

"You're that certain?" Jola asked. "She still might choose Todor or Zora."

"No, she said before she was set on me. I don't think she'll change. If anything, I believe seeing us together, in good and stormy weather, will make her choice the easier." Nefeli eased Jola down. "Are you ready?"

"With you at my side? For anything." Jola stroked Nefeli's cheek.

Nefeli grabbed her hand and twined their fingers. "This is your choice?"

"You doubt?" Jola pulled back, surprise clear on her face.

"No." Nefeli said triple fast. She bit her teeth, then shrugged. "I just want to hear it one more time."

"I love you, and take great pleasure in standing by your side in fair and foul weather."

Tears turned Nefeli's gaze to a crystalline blur. She pulled Jola close. "And I love you, and will have none other at my side."

Before they could kiss for more than a moment, a trumpet blew high on the walls.

And again and again, in a celebratory pattern proclaiming far and wide that the Terparchon and her entourage approached the gates.

Nefeli and Jola rushed into more formal clothes, and layers suitable for standing outside. Attendants came to help them don glittering circlets, and jeweled spangles, but they stole quick caresses whenever they could. Until they finally faced each other, lights sparkling off the precious metals and stones adorning them.

"Let's go face our fate" Nefeli offered her hand.

Jola took it, and the future Marchon and Terparchon headed out to met the current.

26

Cahide preferred safety in numbers. Even a stranger could sometimes hide in a crowd, if it were large enough. Especially if said stranger bowed to local customs and dressed and presented themselves as something close to a neighbor. One never managed it completely without intense study, certainly she never had, but she fancied that the people nearest might consider her odd and not from around here, but also not so strange as to be something to worry about.

Even if this required wearing only two layers—a thick tunic and matching mantle—rather than a proper set of ten or twelve lightweight gowns. Not to mention removing her veil completely and at best covering her hair with another length of thick cloth. Although, truth, she appreciated the warmth the heavier cloth offered given the growing autumnal cool, so different from home.

The same sun shone overhead, but provided so much less warmth. How long since she last spent the colder seasons in the north? Long enough to forget how the chill could settle into bones, or maybe she'd aged and become more sensitive to such matters.

She didn't care for the architecture of Tharis, Codaros's northern capital. The high city walls that were no longer defensible. The many towers people kept adding onto the ridiculous castle. The fireplaces that ate nearly all the heat they produced. On the bright side, someone —reputedly the Marchon—had successfully introduced closed stoves to the castle.

But for an occasion such as the last of the court's return, she'd leave the comfort of her castle room and its wood stove to gather with others.

Alas, she'd also forgotten how much noise and stench a crowd could rouse. The whole city population seemed determined to fill the square in front of the winter palace, leaving only just enough room for the Terparchon and her entourage to make their way through.

Cahide stood atop the ramparts watching the scene from high above, and she had ample company. Noise rose from below, but many of the palace denizens thronged the ramparts with her. Guards, courtiers, servants, all redolent of sweat and onions in their heavy cloth that never washed as thoroughly as they seemed to think.

The Marchon had returned only a day earlier. The portion of court that had traveled with him and that which had gone with Nefeli and Jola mingled together amidst the crowd. Here and there below she could pick out this princess or that compeer, or that scribe, or that minister of trade.

Yet whenever Cahide managed to scan the crowd, which was rarely, all eyes seemed drawn to the center of the courtyard as Nefeli and Jola, with the Marchon behind them, welcomed the Terparchon home.

Cahide had been impressed with Jola even before meeting her, and only more so after. She also

liked Nefeli from what she'd seen of her, especially with her attention to detail.

Most of all, she appreciated how well the two dealt together and their ideas for furthering trade and exchange of information. She'd talked with them often during the weeks traveling up from the southern capital.

They gave her hope for the future with their energy and commitment to the land—and to each other.

Many of the Erevestis Council would like them too, and other as well even if they wouldn't admit it. She'd sent coded letters back to that effect, with no word yet on how they were received.

A breeze eased around her as the crowd shifted to let a woman slip in nearby.

First glance indicated familiarity, but provided no name or context. On second, Cahide recognized Amara, former princess and devoted servant of the Terparchon, all too easily despite the passage of time. Cahide felt much older and knew she looked it. Perhaps Amara had aged, but she barely showed it.

"I've heard interesting things about your visit to the former Shadow." Amara smiled at Cahide, showing her teeth,

There was the woman Cahide remembered, cutting right to the chase. But she didn't begrudge sharing some information. "They did well. Nefeli and Jola Danced such as I've rarely seen in my years— maybe even you in yours?"

A different smile crossed Amara's face, warmer and with less teeth, but as always she failed to rise to the bait.

"I like your land's future—how they grow stronger together." Cahide waved at the two as they bowed to the Terparchon. "It gives me hope."

"They give me hope, too."

And so they stood, shoulder to shoulder, as the Terparchon set proud hands upon her daughter's shoulders and greeted her daughter's love likewise. Nothing was said that day, but few in the crowd—and certainly not either women—failed to guess the announcement soon to come of the Terparchon and Marchon's heirs.

Long live Princess Jola and Compeer Nefeli!

SNEAK PEEK
CHAPTER 1

B e among the first to learn of new releases: sign-up for her newsletter at https://BookHip.com/PCSWMCK. Book recommendations, updates on stories, and snippets from works-in-progress—plus a free Dancing Princesses story for signing up!

The world of the Dancing Princesses continues—read on for a peek at *A Spy Princess*!

Trouble never arrived alone, always as part of a pair. Other members of the court, servants and courtiers, laughed at the notion. Considered it provincial, the kind of thing only someone from one of the tiny towns in the hinterlands might swallow.

Emmi saw no reason not to admit her superstitions and even embrace them. She didn't walk around proclaiming her worries of paired troubles—but she sought out odd numbers wherever possible. She made certain she wore an odd number of clothes: a simple cloth tied around her privates, another supporting her generous breasts, and a plain gray tunic over. The worn hem hit her mid-calf, almost the same color as her taupe skin. Smooth leather sandals covered her feet, tied on with ribbons that wrapped up past the hem. Soft black hair with purple undertones swung around her face, kept short to be less trouble—and save time to be used elsewhere.

The soft gray and yellow striped mantle draped over her tunic complemented her coloring, but also had the insignia of the court woven into the center marking her as an attendant. Valued, of course, for the rulers and most courtiers recognized they wouldn't function without servants, but still one of those who worked mostly in the back halls, particularly at the summer palace complex with its dozens of buildings, hundreds of stairways, and thousands of rooms, whether within walls or plazas open to the air.

Emmi loved the quarter of the year spent at the summer palace. Some might complain about the heat and humidity, and the risk of the horrendous storms that blew up across the lake at the peak of the summer, but not her. True, even this late in the summer sweat slicked her skin and made her hair cling to the sides of her head. But the wide windows placed even, or especially, in stairwells caught and directed breezes to ensure moisture was regularly wicked away.

More important than heat: her closest sibling worked here, having fallen in love with the area. Emmi's place attending at court allowed her to visit with him every year and carry word back to their family in a small town near the northern capital.

Like her brother, Emmi loved how the southern capital burst with color. Nearly every wall bore some type of adornment, usually mosaics formed of myriad tiles that portrayed nature or history. Matching colored stones formed intricate patterns covering the floors. The public rooms always boasted at least one scene of a previous Terparchon or Marchon conquering this territory or making that decree. The back halls were better—brightened with jungles and forests teeming with animal and bird life, or underwater scenes in lakes and rivers showing one array of colorful fish and snails after another.

The stairways might not have mosaics, but they were whitewashed and then painted and repainted, always with different colors and patterns. Giggles and the smell of paint rose from one story below, where the denizens of the children's palace spent the morning hours decorating. Emmi had stopped by for a few moments earlier, and listened to her seven-year-old daughter explain that the tall-eared purple blob she drew was actually a fish with three tails.

A fish who'd last on the stairs for a year or more, delighting—or, more likely, confusing—anyone who noticed. Susa's current best friend, the child of the Terparchon's Chief Accountant, painted a rainbow snail nearby. All children played together regardless of their parents' station, because, as the Terparchon had pointed out more than once in Emmi's hearing, who could tell what a child would be until they were grown? Much as Emmi loved order and tidiness, she preferred her daughter have a world of possibilities before her. There were good reasons she'd left her village to take service, no matter that she still sometimes missed home.

And people who understood that a bad thing that came alone was only waiting for its match to follow.

Emmi counted the steps when climbing to ensure the third floor of the northern administrative hall remained exactly twenty-three above the first. Everything in its place—order above chaos. Her lungs protested the speed with which she'd climbed, so she paused at the top. Tightened the light-blue cord around her waist, adjusting the ends so that they swayed against her hip rather than her front.

No stains marred the fabric, though bits of dust clung to the hem. She'd been summoned halfway through cleaning out the rooms of the three princesses she regularly waited on. Careful with a broom she might be, but one couldn't escape dust.

And she hadn't been allowed time to go back to her rooms to change. The thin, fair-skinned eleee who'd come for her had sworn they were told to take over her tasks—without specifying whether for the morning or permanently. They'd nearly grabbed the broom out of her hand! Then sent her on her way with a smile.

The kind of look that said *better you than me*.

Small wonder she sought out odds to ward off trouble. As she walked down the hall, she brushed her fingers along the nine doors lining the left side, matched on the right but with an extra at the far end to ensure they totaled twenty-one. Transom windows above each door were all partly opened, ensuring ample circulation of warm air.

A glance ahead at the open door of the palacekeeper who oversaw the servants who cleaned, mended, and tended, showed only one person present: Desma herself.

The room seemed small with Desma in it, although it was almost the size of the lesser princess chambers in their hall. Of medium height and breadth, Desma had brown hair liberally streaked with gray, brown eyes, light brown skin, and round features topped by a snub nose.

Every element of Desma's appearance, from polished sandals to light yellow tunic to brighter mantle with the court insignia, individually was unremarkable. The whole somehow became memorable, and Desma stood out whenever she ventured into the royal reception areas as readily as she did against the bare whitewashed walls. The chamber held a table and a stool on either side. Shelves affixed to the wall behind supported assorted piles of scrap paper, several chalk boards, and broken nubs of chalk.

The table held more scraps of paper—and a carafe of spiced water with two dinged bronze goblets.

The presence of refreshment and enough cups made Emmi nervous. So too did the kind but wry twist to Desma's thin lips.

Emmi accepted a glass of water as she perched on a stool, not daring to so much as offer to pour it herself. The metal was cool to the touch, already beading with perspiration indicating the water had started with ice. A single chilly sip, and she set it down with care and awaited her fate.

"How are you and your princesses?" Desma always began with the same question, at least for Emmi ever since she'd come to Desma's attention in the first place and risen to attend princesses. But perhaps Desma had less of a smile than other times?

Or maybe Emmi worried over air fears. "All's well. No troubles to report."

Not in her work. Her daughter complained about the upcoming progress and having to leave Yaras and her beloved uncle-aunt. Emmi's sibling, in turn, regularly bent her ear about her lack of love life. Much as she loved him, he regularly suggested the most unsuitable candidates with whom to break her years-long fast. This one because he had a nice smile, that one had such a neat swing to their hips. Even a man notable mostly for having serenaded a different woman at midnight outside the hall Emmi lived in, waking her daughter and every other child in the building and resulting in cranky parents the next morning.

If anything, serving the princesses offered Emmi a respite from family drama. She was fortunate that the princesses were all easy to please and did much for themselves—yet still appreciated the order and tidiness that Emmi brought to their lives.

With the occasional bobble, but that was only to be expected.

"Gisela is still surprised and a bit uneasy with my keeping her rooms tidy." Emmi winced. The newest princess hadn't fully adjusted to having a servant attend her clothes and chambers. "But she always thanks me for arranging for food and water and having her clothes cleaned. Though I did find her once trying to wash out a mantle herself."

Desma shuddered. "Tell me it was a plain one."

Emmi shook her head. Even the plain dancing tunics of the princesses required a special degree of care to ensure they didn't wear out too fast or get mixed up between sizes, but the mantles with embroidery or fringe needed even more cautious laundering, when they couldn't be spot-cleaned. "No, but she hasn't tried again since."

"Good. I'll have a word with her, if necessary." Desma lifted her cup and made a toast to absent princesses. "But it is so much simpler if they just accept that good laundering requires skilled labor as well as strength. I needn't ask if Jola or Heron has tried to clean their clothes lately."

"They never would. Of course Jola is rarely in her room anyway, and doesn't require that much assistance from me these days."

"That is a consideration for reallocating assignments." Desma nodded. "I know you've lent a hand many times to your fellows in keeping up with their princesses."

Both were well aware of where Jola spent most of her days and nights, in royal chambers with her lover. Just one reason Emmi was able to pitch in and help others.

"And Heron?"

"They're as lovely to serve as ever." Emmi folded her hands in her lap, hoping no blush stained her cheeks. She'd helped Heron, a stranger made princess, adjust to Codaros in their first years. Explaining Codaros customs while she cleaned had grown into a tradition of trading stories several times a week.

"Good, though I am not surprised." Desma made a note on a scrap of paper. "They've been part of court long enough to know the rules. Gisela will learn, she seems intelligent enough."

Emmi nodded, waiting for the trouble to descend.

Desma stared down at the paper in front of her. It had many lines written, half crossed out, and nearly all impossible to read upside-down no matter how Emmi tried.

The other woman said nothing, letting the pause spiral out into something bigger until Emmi couldn't handle the quiet.

"Is there any change to the splitting of the court?" Emmi asked. "There are so many rumors going around that there will be three small courts rather than two this year."

"Rumor does seem to have the right of it this time, but that needn't trouble you." Desma set her stylus down and clasped hands. "I can say no more at this time, but you will be following the Marchon's train on southern and eastern progress."

South. Warmer and slower than the north, for Emmi had enough experience with both. If she had a preference it was the south. Beautiful, hot, and with some slow, rough patches through the occasional jungle, and lots of hilly country.

"You're doing excellent work." Desma smiled, showing her teeth. "I wish I had more such as you in employ."

"Yes?"

"You handle three princesses with ease, sometimes as many as five in a pinch, with no difficulties. Alas, I have other staff unable to care for a single person."

Dread roiled in Emmi's belly. She took a second sip of spiced water, but it did nothing to ease her nerves. The cup rocked when she returned it to the table, despite her care.

"I need you to switch for the fall progress. We can reconsider when we reach the winter palace, if necessary, but not before."

Of course Desma would follow the Terparchon's progress to the north. That part made sense, even though one of Desma's deputies would accompany the southern progress and be able to make changes. But whatever Emmi was to take on, Desma didn't want her abandoning it early or at all.

"Switch to . . ." Emmi started, only to trail off.

Desma's smile still showed her teeth, but her gaze turned pensive. "It's not a big change, from three princesses to a single compeer—and a royal compeer at that!"

A royal compeer? There were three, four if one counted the Marchon, but surely he wouldn't need Emmi. He had an attendant who'd served him as long as Emmi had been at court. As for his and the Terparchon's children, each had mixed reputations among the lower halls. The elder daughter, Nefeli, was a born compeer and always knew where people were, which could be a bit unnerving. Todor, the middle child, had memory issues and reputedly would tell one servant something and assume others knew it. Zora, the younger daughter, tended to lose things and throw fits until they were found.

"Who?" Emmi asked.

"Zora." Desma reached over and patted Emmi's hand. "You can tell your princesses today that you're leaving them, and first thing tomorrow we'll make the change. I'll assign a fine attendant or two to take over with them, and I'll show you around Zora's chambers myself."

"Do I have a choice?" Emmi racked her memory for tales of Zora from the servants' halls. Surprisingly few, other than her possessiveness.

"Emmi." Was that a plea in Desma's voice? "I'm near the end of possibilities. Zora's previous attendant suited for years, but reached her thirty while on the spring march and retired. Since then, she's gone through . . . nine attendants."

"Nine?" Two or three might be understandable after such a long time with the same person, but thrice that number said a lot about a person.

"No one has lasted a full moon." Desma sighed.

"What happened?" At three or four moons total since the retirement, most wouldn't have even lasted a half-moon.

"Didn't like the condition of her rooms, didn't like her reaction to them tidying, complaints of inconsistency—of her asking for things and then countermanding the orders or denying she'd given them—and dislike of her, er, companions." Desma counted off on her fingers. "On the other side, complaints of prying, unreliability, sticking their noses where they weren't wanted."

And Desma wanted Emmi to wade into this and make it all right?

"You're the most capable person I have." Desma laid her hands flat on the table. "There are one or two attendants back at Tharis who might do to sub in when we get there, though no promises, but at a minimum I need someone to see to her on the autumn progress who can stick with it—no complaints on either side. I have no one else with the experience, the subtlety, the diplomacy."

"Experience?" Many others with far more years service than Emmi, plus ample subtlety and diplomacy.

"You have a sibling who's a multiple, don't you?"

"Yes." Emmi sat back, gripping the edge of the stool. That was why Desma wanted her? "You think that's why she's hard to please? But my brother-sister is the sweetest, kindest person I know."

"It might help," Desma said. "I don't know how many people Zora is, but some of them are harder to deal with than others, and your familiarity . . ."

Emmi tried to offer alternatives, but Desma had an objection for every one. It was a polite fiction between them, Desma offering Emmi the illusion of choice. They both knew in the end she'd have to accept the change.

No matter how Emmi considered the matter, even though the new position came with a pay raise, it was a piece of bad news.

One, no doubt, with the match waiting around a corner to pounce.

Still, Emmi was allowed to tell her current princesses. She'd have a last exchange with one in particular, who'd been a painful joy to wait upon. One last time to look on Heron close up, talk to them about their day, see them smile just for her.

Then never again.

ABOUT THE AUTHOR

Never miss a book! Visit A.R. Henle's webpage, www.arhenle.com, and sign up for her newsletter, for quarterly updates, sneak peeks, and free stories.

A.R. Henle writes non-fiction by day and fiction by night. Magical realism, fantasy, fantasy romance—and history!

www.ingramcontent.com/pod-product-compliance
Lightning Source LLC
Chambersburg PA
CBHW061443210726
48287CB00007B/2329